D0960913

Also by Rob Thomas:

Satellite Down
Doing Time: Notes from the Undergrad
Slave Day
Rats Saw God

GREEN THUMB

ROB THOMAS

Simon & Schuster Books for Young Readers

THANKS TO RUSSELL SMITH, JENNIFER ROBINSON,
JENNY ZIEGLER, BOB AND DIANA THOMAS,
JOHN RUDOLPH, MIKE CONATHAN, ARI GREENBURG, AND,
FOR HIS PATIENCE AND PERSISTENCE, DAVID GALE

SIMON & SCHUSTER BOOKS FOR YOUNG READERS
An imprint of Simon & Schuster Children's Publishing Division
1230 Avenue of the Americas
New York, New York 10020
Text copyright © 1999 by Rob Thomas
All rights reserved including the right of reproduction in whole or in part in any form.
SIMON & SCHUSTER BOOKS FOR YOUNG READERS is a trademark of
Simon & Schuster.

Book design by Anahid Hamparian
The text for this book is set in 11-point Matt Antique.
Printed and bound in the United States of America
10 9 8 7 6 5 4 3 2 1

Library of Congress Cataloging-in-Publication Data
Thomas, Rob.
Green Thumb / Rob Thomas. — 1st ed.
p.   cm.
Summary: While spending the summer in the Amazon rain forest of Brazil doing botani-
cal research, thirteen-year-old Grady discovers a secret language used by the trees to
communicate with each other and falls afoul of the dictatorial Dr. Carter, whose
motives seem questionable.
ISBN 0-689-81780-0
[1. Rain forests—Fiction. 2. Amazon River Valley—Fiction.
3. Brazil—Fiction. 4. Environmental protection—Fiction.
5. Indians of South America—Brazil—Fiction.] I. Title.
PZ7.T36935Gr 1999
[Fic]—dc21
98-39992
CIP
AC

FIRST EDITION

For Greg McCormack . . . Purple Dot!

Bobby Ross edges in closer to me, but there's nowhere for me to escape since Ed Stimmons has parked his wide self right behind me. Bobby drapes his pitching arm over the top of my locker. He's so close, I can smell the peanut butter he had for lunch. Chunky, by the look of his gums.

"So Grady, can we count on you, buddy?" Bobby says. He tries to force out a smile, but he doesn't show any teeth, and it ends up looking more like a smirk. "We gotta stay eligible for baseball, you know."

Try studying then, moron.

I think it; I don't say it. I'm not stupid. What I say is . . .

"It's pretty late for tutoring, but if you have any questions, I'll try to help. Is there something in particular? Fossils?"

That's not the kind of help they're asking for, but I want to make them say the words. I hate guys like this—the ones who still have delusions that they're decent people because they're not drug dealers or arsonists, and for some unexplainable reason, teachers find them charming.

"Naw, man," says Bobby. "It's Mrs. Washington's tests. They're impossible."

If they were impossible, I wouldn't have a ninety-nine average, but I decide not to point this out either. My confused look is probably no more believable than Bobby's smile, but I take it out for a test drive anyway.

"So what are you saying?" I ask.

Bobby looks at Ed. They don't want to have to spell it out for me.

"You don't have to do anything, Grady. Just play it loose with your cover sheet."

"Be cool, man," adds Ed.

"We won't forget it. We'll owe you one," says Bobby.

Like either one of them have anything I want. What are they going to do? Ask me to be their pal? Right. Maybe they'll throw in the requisite lobotomy too.

"We'll even miss a couple," Bobby says.

"On purpose," Ed tacks on. I laugh—on the inside.

"I don't know," I say. "I didn't study much for this one. You might want to ask somebody else."

Now it's my turn to smirk. Who else are they going to ask?

"See, this is why no one likes you, Grady," Bobby says. "Can't you just be cool for once."

"No one likes me?" I whisper. I shake my head and cover my face with both of my hands like this news upsets me. "All right, you guys," I say, letting my voice begin to quiver. "Just promise me you won't make it too obvious."

When I get home from school, my mom's in the living room talking to the ferns. She doesn't hear me enter the living room, so I just stand there listening. Someday I'm going to get this on tape and sell it to *America's Funniest Home Videos*.

"And I told her that if you keep giving her money, if you don't cut her off, she's never going to learn to fend for herself, but Mom says, 'Connie, she's my daughter, she's your sister, we can't just give up on her.'"

Hilarious. She even does Grandma's warbly voice for the ferns. I can't help laughing. Mom turns around, embarrassed.

"I didn't hear you come in, honey."

"I've told you you're wasting your time, Mom. They're plants. They'll grow for you if you get their pH level right, if they get enough sun, just enough water. They don't care about Aunt Clarice's gambling problem."

"They don't seem to mind hearing about it," she says. "It must be a boring life—a plant's— sitting in the same place all the time."

Mom's not a kook. She just plays one at home.

She sticks her finger into the soil of one of the ferns and touches it to her tongue. One day I'm going to come home and find her chanting over voodoo dolls. "How was school today?"

"Boring. Simple. Permissive. My brain is starting to rot. I can feel it."

"We talked about this. There's just not enough money to keep sending you to private school. You'll have to start making the best of it."

"They're all idiots."

"They can't all be bad, Grady. Why don't you invite someone over to spend the night . . . or the weekend. I'm sure they'd love to see your greenhouse."

"Mom, do you remember junior high at all? My greenhouse? Maybe if I had a 64-bit Sega Genesis and a library of games out there, then they'd like to see it. Maybe if I were performing an alien autopsy rather than plant growth experiments."

Mom puts her hands on her hips. She truly believes I'm missing out on something. "What about the flytrap? Everyone loves that."

"I'll ask around," I say. I cup my hands around my mouth and pretend I'm wandering around the cafeteria. "Hey! Anyone want to come over and spend the weekend? See insects eaten alive!"

"I'll bet you'd have some takers."

"Real winners, I'm sure."

Mom sets down her water pitcher and

wipes her hands on an apron. "Did I tell you," she begins, "what the Hyde Park Players chose for our summer produc—"

"Did I get any mail?" I ask.

"It's by the phone."

Mail is one of my favorite parts of my day. I've been grand champion two years running at the National Science Fair. Now it seems like something arrives daily: an invitation to participate in a university study on gifted students; interview requests from academic journals; mostly I receive information from colleges. There isn't an Ivy League school that hasn't offered me a scholarship yet, and I'm only thirteen.

Today there are three envelopes addressed to me. I tear open the first one while Mom provides background noise by droning on about her theater group.

". . . we decided on *Arsenic and Old Lace*. Gerta Lupinski made quite a case for *Cat on a Hot Tin Roof*, but cooler heads thought it best if . . ."

I tune her out and scan the first letter. It's from a company that makes CD-ROM encyclopedias. They've sent the beta version and they want me to sign a form that says I use their product. They'll put my name on some list to impress people when they market it to schools. I pull out the CD but trash the rest of it.

". . . for sure that I'll be doing the costumes for some of it, but I think I'm going to also audition for the part of . . ."

Opening the second envelope, I turn slightly away from my yapping mother. This one is an actual letter. It's from Diwakar Vishwakarma. He's president of the Young Scientists Association and a certifiable nutcake. Sure, D. V.'s won just about every prize there is out there, and he had two pharmaceutical patents by the time he was nineteen, but now he's this joke. The rest of us call him "Cause." He's always got one, and he wants the Young Scientists to throw all their energy into whatever it is. This time it's cosmetic testing on animals. His note to me is handwritten, and he's sent along photographs—cats with their eyelids removed, scabby rabbits with most of their fur gone. *Okay, Cause, you win. Starting today I'm boycotting the whole line of Sensuelle Elustra cosmetics and hair-care products.* I toss the packet.

My mom, God bless her, still isn't winded.

". . . so Mary says to me, 'Don't you think I'd be perfect as Abby Brewster,' when she knows very well that that's the part I might want, and she's really better for the part of Martha."

The return address on the final envelope—a big manila one that feels like it has a videotape in it—reads EMBRYO. I've never heard of it. That *usually* means it's a waste of my time, but I open it anyway.

> Mr. Jacobs,
>
> Congratulations. You are one of six students in the United States invited to participate in an exciting new program—The Embryo Project.
>
> The Embryo Project is unlike any advanced scientific study program ever offered to young people. Made possible by a combined grant from Pacific Oil and Landslide Communications, Embryo's goal is to give the most promising young scientists a chance to work in symbiotic partnership with some of the greatest scientific minds at work today.
>
> But Embryo isn't stopping there. Because the keys to the natural world's timeless mysteries lie in applied research, Embryo's classes won't be confined by four walls. Instead, our four worldwide "classrooms" will be the Mars-landing simulators of NASA, the rich archaeological mother lodes of Egypt, the McDonald Observatory in far West Texas, and the rain forests of Brazil.
>
> In view of your obvious aptitude for botanical research, we're

inviting you to join Embryo's Wood Stock Project, a revolutionary rain forest regeneration program now taking place in the Brazilian Amazon Basin. Full details on Wood Stock can be found in the enclosed tape and brochure.

Best of all, Grady, the entire cost of your travel, lodging, and food will be paid by the donor companies. You'll be back home in plenty of time to begin your fall classes. And because we consider it our . . .

"Mom," I say, interrupting her tirade about all the vulgar language playwrights insist on using these days, "I'm going to Brazil."

2

Bobby Ross sits a row behind me in earth science, but I hear his whispered threat clearly.

"After school today. You die."

I glance down at the test Mrs. Washington had just handed back. A big red zero was circled in red felt tip. She'd scrawled a message beside the score—*see me after class.*

Once the bell rings I try to get out of here without talking to her, but she snags me by the shoulder and orders me to wait "just one minute." After the other students clear out, she sits back down at her desk. "Are you going to tell me what happened?" she asks.

"What do you mean?"

"Do you mind telling me why a student of your caliber intentionally tanked a major test?"

"I'm still making an A. Even with the zero, I have a ninety-one test average for the semester and a ninety-five homework average. Besides, grades don't really count until high school."

Junior high teachers hate it when you say stuff like that to them. "That doesn't answer my question, Grady."

I look at her.

"Maybe I can help fill in the blanks," she said. "Mr. Ross and Mr. Stimmons, both of whom sit behind you, recorded similar scores with remarkably similar answers. Did you know they were copying off you?"

"No."

"Grady, it's okay. You can tell me. I'll let you take the test over. The other boys have already gotten what's coming to them."

"I just didn't study much, Mrs. Washington," I say. "It won't happen again."

She shakes her head and stares at me like she's expecting me to squeal, but that's not me. I take care of my own problems.

"Is that all?" I ask. "Can I go?"

I assume I'll run into Bob and Ed somewhere between my last class, algebra, and the bus circle. They don't disappoint me. They're blocking the sidewalk that runs behind the gym. Ed is clenching and unclenching his fists, but of course, it's Bobby who speaks.

"We're off the baseball team, thanks to you," he says.

"Look," I say, "do we have to talk about this? Why not just get it over with. Is one of you going to hold my arms while the other punches, or is it going to be more of a tag team thing?"

I guess they hadn't worked out the details, because they kind of glance at each other.

"Why don't you flip a coin," I suggest.

With that, Ed, the bigger of the two, loses his temper and throws a fist at my mouth. It knocks me down. I can tell my lip's bleeding. Above me, the ubiquitous fight crowd starts to ring the participants. I'm afraid they're going to be pretty dissatisfied. I roll over from my back to my stomach and pick myself up.

"Not so funny now, is it?" Ed screams. "Is it?"

"If you could've hit a baseball that hard, maybe I would've let you cheat," I say.

This time he slugs me in the stomach, but it's Bobby who does the talking. "See how no one is jumping in to break this up? Anyone else in school and at least one person would call a teacher or even try to help you out. But no one's going to help you."

I speak once I catch my breath. "So I guess I won't get to play any of your reindeer games, huh? Why don't you two go shower together? Oh, that's right, you're not on the team together anymore. I guess that's why you're so mad now."

A few people laugh, but I don't get to feel proud of myself for very long. Bobby launches himself at me, tackling me. My head slams back hard on the concrete sidewalk. The first two punches he throws I don't even feel, though I know he's connecting because blood is filling my mouth. Some remote understanding of the situation tells me I'm on the verge of losing consciousness. He's got me pinned to the ground with his knees on my shoulders. He's saying something, but my comprehension is delayed until maybe a second after I see his lips move.

"Hey, if you're so smart, what are you doing on the ground like this? What good is that brain of yours now? What's the matter? Nothing to say anymore? You're not going to cry, are you?"

I spit a mouthful of blood at him.

"Now you are," he screams. He's over the edge. "Now you're going to cry. You're not getting up until you cry for me."

He lands a punch, and I think I feel a tooth loosen. I see him raise his fist again. I brace for the impact, but I refuse to close my eyes. If he's going to keep this up until I cry, we're going to be here a long time.

But the blow never comes. A giant hand swoops down and catches Bobby's fist. It's Joe Maldonado. People call him Joe the Volcano. He pulls Bobby off me, holding on to no part of Bobby but his fist. Ed starts to say something, but Joe cuts him off. "Are you going to start kicking the cheerleaders' butts when you're done here?" he says.

I want to object. I've just been insulted—he's comparing beating me up to beating up cheerleaders—but I'm not quite able to talk yet. Joe stands above my body. I see a look pass between the two baseball players, a moment where they try to decide whether, together, they could take Joe. Joe sees it, too. "Be smart," he says.

The crowd that's gathered is silent. Bobby, the brains of the dull-namic duo, attempts to laugh it off. "Aw man, Joe. It's cool. I was just about done with the wuss anyway." He turns to Ed. "C'mon, we're gonna miss the bus."

And that's that. The crowd disperses, and I'm left there on the ground, bloody but not defeated. Joe the Volcano offers me a hand up, but I roll over to my stomach and push myself up on my own. I don't need anybody's help.

I walk home. The back of my head is stinging. I touch my hair back there, and I'm not surprised that there's blood on my fingers. I keep spitting blood onto the sidewalk. I can't believe I'm having to deal with this neanderthal schoolyard-brawling scene. I mean, this isn't some Arkansas hillbilly backwater. It's Westwood, one of the safer places to live in LA.

I don't even consider telling my father. That would just lay the groundwork for further encounters with the Bash Brothers. Anyway, it's not like Dad would actually do anything. He's not the Steven Seagal type; he's a professor of physics at UCLA. Maybe not for long, though. In the eighties, he received these huge grants to work on "Star Wars," a missile defense system they were designing for outer space. After they discontinued that project, the university wanted him to continue his work because they thought it could be applied to air traffic control, but Dad essentially researched himself out of a job, because he proved that the principles he'd devised for radar missile detection wouldn't work with the relatively slow and gigantic commercial airplanes. Last year the university denied him tenure. That means we'll probably be moving again. If he were still bringing in millions of dollars to the university, they wouldn't have done that to him. It's all so political. If I were Dad, I would've just lied when they asked about the radar, told them what they wanted to hear. He could've kept getting those fat grants for another decade. Maybe then I'd still be in private school.

I don't even go into the house when I get home—I have no desire to watch Mom wig out when she sees me. I head straight out to the greenhouse that Dad and I built nearly four years ago. It was my tenth-birthday present. I work the combinations of all three locks on the door, step inside, and flip on the light switch and my 500-square-foot lab is illuminated. This is home. This is where I work, my real school. Another botanist would look around in here and understand almost immediately what's so special about what I do in here. A lay person—just about anyone else—would just think I have a lot of mock orange trees. But if they looked closer, maybe they would notice something odd—and not just that they're exceptionally healthy plants. (I challenge you to find one leaf on the floor in here.) Nope. There's something more. You have to look closely.

They're all exactly alike. They're duplicates of each other.

I've cloned them.

Thirty-six trees and they've all got a small knot 11 centimeters below the first branch. There are ninety-two leaves on each tree. They're all 1.12 meters tall. But there's more: They're engineered. Genetically designed. They've got a specific duty. Someday an army of these trees will line the highways of America. Why? Because they're tough. I've made them that way. These guys laugh at carbon monoxide. They thrive in a drought, flourish in a monsoon. They'll survive all but the hardest of freezes.

Someday they're going to make me rich. In December, they're going to make me the first three-time grand champion at the National Science Fair. I look at them, and sometimes I feel like a god.

Before I get to work, I look at myself in the mirror above the sink. My lower lip looks like a dangling sausage. My right eye is nearly closed, and both eyes are ringed in black. That's all right. I wasn't much to look at before the fight. I've got this round Charlie Brown head, partly because of my cheeks. I'm not exactly fat. It's more like I'm soft. My grandma calls all my cousins Sweetie. Me, she calls Puddin'. That says a lot. My whole person—my cheeks, my gut, my arms—all have this sort of soft, tapioca consistency. I know enough about genetics not to blame myself for it. It's not like I'm scarfing down buckets of fried chicken and bags of Reese's Pieces. I eat like everyone else eats. I've seen pictures of Dad at my age. Same basic look as mine, except that I ended up with Mom's green eyes and dark brown hair. My hair is long most of the time, but it's not some kind of statement. Cutting it's just never high on my priority list. It's not like some stylish haircut is going to thrust me into the world of lunchroom handholders and mall-cruising trendsetters.

I splash water on my face before beginning my daily ritual: watering, measuring, analyzing, recording. I flip on my computer monitor in order to plug in the new data. A message at the top tells me I have e-mail. I click on the icon. The dialog box indicates it's from Dr. Phillip Carter, the lead researcher for the rain forest study—The Wood Stock Project is what they call it. Dad and I talked for a long time over the weekend about the trip, but whether or not I could go was never really in question despite Mom carrying on like a harpy, inventing all these deadly scenarios in which she'd never see me again. "He's thirteen!" she kept saying, like that meant something. Dad just wanted me to look at all the angles. He wondered whether I would miss spending the summer around people my own age.

"Hardly," I told him.

Maybe I should explain something about myself. My earliest memory is of the *Challenger* space shuttle blowing up. I was two at the time, and Mom always thinks I imagined it, or that I remember it from seeing it later on video, but I know what I saw, and what I felt. All my toys were spaceships back then, and I dreamed about going into outer space. To this day I have dreams about being one of the people on the *Challenger*, but the weird thing is that it's not a nightmare. In the dream, I know it's going to crash. I know I'm going to die, but my life is somehow complete, because I'm doing exactly what I want. Exploring. Discovering.

Until I was nine or so, I planned on being an astronaut. Then I found out that my 20/40 vision was going to keep that from ever happening. Besides, by then I'd figured out that I'm a lot happier when I'm not around other people. I like working by myself. Being by myself, really. Botany seemed like the thing. Plants don't talk to you. There are no protesters out there telling you you shouldn't be testing on that potato.

I click open the mail from Dr. Carter.

Mr. Jacobs,
The people at Embryo were good enough to send me a copy of the report that accompanied your "Maximum Shade/Minimum Sunlight" championship project from last year's National Science Fair. Very impressive. We're looking forward to having you down here. If you haven't yet, you will

```
soon be receiving a packet of information
about rain forest ecosystems. Please make
sure you've thoroughly familiarized your-
self with it before you leave. We want
you to be ready to hit the ground run-
ning. I assume you have a laptop computer.
If not, get one and bring it. You'll need
a fast IBM-compatible with at least a 2-
gig hard drive. E-mail me your final
flight reservations. One of your future
coworkers will meet you in Belém. Look for
a sign with your name on it. Get a
Portuguese phrase book. It'll come in
handy.
— P. C.
```

At first I thought I'd lie about why my face looks like this, but Dad came home for dinner, which is rare, so I figured I'd better tell the truth. Or at least something close to it.

"I got in a fight," I say, once he asks.

"What was the cause of this altercation?" Dad asks as he ladles himself some more gravy.

Yes, I know. He talks like a geek.

"The guy said something mean about this girl in my class," I say, knowing this reason will make him happy.

"Did you get in a couple shots?" my father asks.

"He knows he was in a fight."

I can almost hear the wheels a-churning in my mother's head. "Is this a girl you're fond of, Gra—?"

"Did you get it sorted out?" asks Dad, cutting her off.

"Oh yeah, we're buddies now," I say.

And he believes me, because that's the way things should be. Boys will be boys. They'll get in fights for stupid reasons and then run off and play stickball together. It's like my father thinks the whole world is an episode of *Happy Days*.

Dad is a huge man. When I was little, I used to imagine that, because of his size, most people were probably afraid of him. I know I was. But since I've gotten older and I've seen how the world works, I know that's not the case. Though he probably tips the scale close to three hundred, I doubt Dad could lift anything much heavier than his dinner plate. If I'm Puddin', he's General Custard. Not just in body type either. I've seen how he gets bullied around all the time by students of his, by the head of his department, by the UCLA administration. People who aren't nearly as smart as he is.

As soon as we're done with our turkey, Mom clears the plates and scoops us each helpings of ice cream.

"So, Grady," she says as she sets the bowl in front of me, "is this girl cute?"

Dad saves me from having to answer. "I talked to some of my colleagues about your Dr. Carter today," he says. "He's got quite a reputation among his peers."

"Good or bad?" I ask.

Dad pauses with his spoon right up next to his mouth. A bead of chocolate sauce drips onto his sleeve as he considers his response.

"He's supposed to be good," Dad says, "but his reputation owes more to his unconventional methods and his personality than to the works he's published. They say the people who work for him refuse to work with anyone else afterward, that he's some sort of cult figure. A few of the UCLA botany professors suggested I should be a bit leery of sending you."

"You already said I—," I begin.

"And you can. I'm just offering a warning. They say he works his people very hard. They're in the field by dawn, not back until it's dark. I hope you're not expecting a vacation. Remember, three months is a long time."

"I'll be fine," I say.

"So what are you going to do about your project?"

I've been so excited about the trip that I hadn't even thought about it. The National Science Fair isn't for another nine months, but if I have any chance at winning it all again, then I should have my research done by the end of September, a month before the local qualifying fair. After that it should just be a matter of writing up the findings and making some sort of display that catches a judge's attention. Wait until school starts to begin your research and you end up looking like those slackers who are required to enter because they've signed up for a high school honors science class. They're the ones with the little six-turn rat maze projects that seek to determine whether a rat responds better to Swiss, cheddar, or Limburger. Contests hardly get challenging until the state level. How my research can continue is a pretty major stumbling block to my leaving. I look at my Dad.

"I don't suppose—"

"Don't even think it," he says. "I spend fourteen hours a day in a lab as it is. I don't want to spend an additional ninety minutes in the greenhouse every day."

"I've got plenty of time to—," Mom blurts out.

"C'mon, Dad. You've got to," I say. "You can get that time down to less than an hour after you do it for a couple weeks."

Dad has turned his attention to the bottom of his ice-cream bowl. He responds while spooning out the chocolatey, melted goo from the bottom.

"Even at an hour it's too much. You need to find somebody else."

"I'll do it," says Mom.

"Mom," I say, "it's science."

"It's just measuring stuff and writing it down," she says. "At least, I suspect that's all you want me to do."

I look at Dad. He shrugs.

It's pretty clear that I don't have an option.

I have a premonition that bad things await on the morning after the baseball team wins the league championship. An omen arrives via the morning announcements. The principal orders an afternoon assembly to honor our brave gladiators. After lunch, the baseball players get to sit up on the stage while the band plays and the cheerleaders scream and their coach tells us all what fine young men they are. I'm sitting in the back row of the stands thinking how no one must have told the principal when I won the district, state, and National Science Fair titles last year. Either that or I must have been sick the day they had a pep rally honoring me.

Anyway.

The pep rally must have put my two science colleagues into a foul mood. They weren't up on stage getting their hosannas, so they decide to take it out on me. On our way back to class, they jump me from behind, reach down into my jeans, and grab my underwear. Here I am, weeks from being a high school student, and I'm still getting wedgied. But this is more than a jolly prank wedgie. They want to hurt me. They have me by either side and they manage to lift me all the way off the ground. The fabric digs into parts of me too sensitive to talk about. I don't give them any satisfaction, though. I keep an uninterested look on my face and don't make a peep. The only thing audible is the sound of ripping Hanes and the giggles of bimbo girls who stand there thinking how clever these two hunky meatheads are.

Someday, I think, *I'll look out my panoramic*

office window and watch these two dolts, clad in matching orange jumpsuits, leaf-blowing the grounds of my corporate headquarters. I'll make a note to myself to have my chief groundskeeper chew them out for clocking in seven minutes late and failing to put rubber warning cones around their work area. . . .

But this time I'm not letting it slide. At home that night, I hollow out a Bic disposable pen and lie on my bed practicing my spit wad accuracy. I drill my Einstein-on-bicycle poster eight hundred times with increasingly large spit wads. I make a game out of it. I shoot while diving into the bed. I spin and fire like it's a gunfight. I aim for specific anatomy on Albert. I have to be good, because they're going to want to kill me.

I practice like this for a couple days. In the meantime, I'm following Bobby and Ed around school. I memorize their class schedules, take note of available sniper positions. I prepare a Sucrets case with preassembled spit wads, already formfitted for the cylinder. Most importantly, the tissue-based wads are drenched in my mother's Nair hair removal cream.

Finally, with six days of school remaining, I put the plan into action.

Taking cover where I can find it on campus, I start nailing Bobby and Ed in the back of the head between classes. At first, they seem to think they're imagining things. They run their hands through their hair, look around with their usual confused expressions, then strut away, shoulders pulled back, like "Even dumbfounded, ain't I cool." They don't fully realize what's going on until day two, but by then, I've probably hit each of them three or four times. I always shoot when they're walking in crowds. The bozos spin around, desperate to figure out where the attack is coming from. Ed actually knocks down some tiny sixth-grader walking behind him. Then he frisks the kid. My prey are now so amusingly paranoid, they're more fun to watch than to shoot. They travel down the hallways with their eyes darting back and forth, then, out of the blue, spin like they're trying to catch someone. The sixth time I shoot Bobby, he spots Darcy Ratliff sucking on a pen. He runs over and yanks it out of her mouth, pulling her retainer out with it. Mr. Daniels, the social studies teacher, witnesses this, whips out a referral form, and sends Bobby to the office. I watch from my hiding place in the janitorial closet. Then, as he's pushing out of the huge double doors, I poke my weapon out of the grill in the bottom of the door and pop him in the back of the head from a full fifteen yards away.

"I'm going to kill whoever's doing that when I catch him!" he screams. The people in the hallway who are still loitering after the retainer incident just stare at Bobby like he's escaped the Special Needs classroom.

By Day Three of Operation Payback, my prey is wishing the students of Northshores Junior High were allowed to wear caps, because the collateral damage is starting to show. It isn't exactly obvious, but if you know what you're looking for, you can see the small patches where each thug's hair is starting to thin out. I peg them each three more times during the course of the day.

The weekend gives them a forty-eight hour respite. I spend my final Saturday and Sunday in America packing and showing Mom how to do everything out in the greenhouse. Normally I don't allow her in there, so giving her the combinations to all the padlocks isn't easy. I even show her how she can e-mail me if anything goes wrong.

"Now Mom," I say as I switch off the computer. "This isn't the same as the houseplants. Don't *try* anything. If they're going to die, let them. Don't give them extra water. Don't use one of those "miracle" plant foods. Don't even talk to them."

Mom grinned.

"So you admit that talking to them makes them grow?"

"No," I said. "I'm afraid they'll die of boredom."

Mom looks at me for a moment and cocks her head. "You can be very mean sometimes, Grady."

I sigh. She always takes things personally.

"Look, I'm sor—"

But she's out the door before I can finish.

People think that because I'm smart, I must like school. That's not true at all. School may be easy, but it's almost too easy. It's boring. So what I'm stuck with is spending eight hours a day, five days a week around people who consider armpit noise high comedy. Teachers hate me because I intimidate them. Other kids hate me because I don't blend in nicely. So, given the option, I'd never show up. I'd stay at home, work in the greenhouse, surf the Net, e-mail the few people I've met who I consider my peers, and just hang out until I'm old enough to drive or go to college. That's why Monday is such an unexpected treat. It's the one day in three years of junior high that I wouldn't have traded for any others. I'm sitting by myself at the long end of a lunchroom table when the first school bell rings. I shuffle out with the masses, heading toward Mr. Sokoff's algebra class. That's when I spot Ed Stimmons wearing a Dodgers cap. That might not sound important, but, remember, we're not allowed to wear caps at school, indoors or out. He's heading in a different direction than me, but I alter my course and follow. The payoff is quick. Before he even gets into the main classroom building, Mrs. Brooks, one of the assistant principals, shouts at him. "Ed Stimmons! You know the rules!"

She pantomimes removing a cap.

Ed looks around. He might be able to turn on the jock charm with some of the teachers here, but he knows better than to try it with Mrs. Brooks. He reluctantly pulls off his cap and tries to hunch his shoulders up to make his head disappear into his collar, but it's no good. I see it. So does everyone else standing nearby. The back of his head is a checkerboard of bald and hairy spots. One of Ed's muscled-up buds slaps him on the back and speaks way too loud for Ed's sake. "Yo, dude! Lose a fight with a lawn mower?"

The crowd hee-haws.

"It looks like a disease," said one of the girls. "Like leprosy or something."

Which is a stupid thing for her to say—it doesn't look a thing like leprosy—but the hopeless look on Ed Stimmons's face is priceless. He looks like he might sob.

I don't see Bobby Ross all day, so I know he can't be in much better shape.

The last day of school is pretty much of a waste of time. Teachers make us do all their cleaning for them while they call us up one at a time to get our grades and return our textbooks. I haven't bothered to hunt down either of my nemeses yet. I figure they're blowing the day off, praying their hair will grow back during the summer, but seconds before the bell, they enter earth science.

And they're bald.

They've just decided to shave it all.

People don't laugh this time—this is just too weird—but everyone sure is staring. There's absolute silence as they stroll back toward their seats.

"What're you lookin' at?" Bobby demands of Ben Creighton, this skinny spaz.

"N-n-n-n-nothin'," Ben says, cowering. Bobby walks by him and fakes like he's going to throw a punch. Ben covers his head, and Bobby snorts out a laugh.

"That sure must've been killer lice," I say loud enough for everyone in class to hear.

"Oh, you want some of this?" Bobby says.

I hear him, but I'm not sure if anyone else does, because the room is loud with laughter. They do see him throw the desk between us over on its side. So does Mrs. Washington, who orders him up to the front of the room. I watch as she writes out a referral. Ed sits down behind me. He's whispering just loud enough for me to hear. "Your ass is grass. After school. Your ass is grass."

"Hey, I'm just having fun with you, Ed," I say. "Seriously, I think this Dalai Lama look is really working for you. I don't know, it's kind of . . . spiritual or something."

Stimmons knits his brow as if he's trying to decide whether the Official Bully Code of Conduct permits him to beat me up for an insult he doesn't understand. What a peabrain! He doesn't even suspect that I'm the reason he's shiny on top; he's just looking for someone to take his humiliation out on. Better me than Ben Creighton. At least I can take it. Ben would end up in therapy wondering what he did to deserve it.

After school, while other "students" are screaming and throwing their papers out of their lockers and into the air, I walk my normal course to the bus circle. I'm expecting the tap on my shoulder at any second, but it never comes. I guess Bobby and Ed are enjoying the revelry so much that they've forgotten their duties as school bullies. My lucky day.

I climb on bus No. 16 and grab a seat next to an open window. I take my last look at Northshores Junior High, savoring the fact that I'll never have to return. That's when I spot them—Bobby and Ed. They're coming down the line of buses, hopping up and looking in the windows. Searching for me, I'm sure. They're still two buses behind us when Mr. Jones, the driver, turns over the engine and pulls the sliding door shut. The buses in front of us are starting to pull out of the lot. Bobby and Ed are now a bus behind us, but they're really moving. My bus starts to roll. Bobby jogs up alongside and spots me.

"There he is," he shouts to Ed. He keeps an easy pace alongside the bus and reaches up and slams his palm against my window.

"You're lucky! But you can't hide all summer," he yells.

But he's wrong. I'm leaving in four hours on a plane for Brazil. Maybe I'll regret this next year on the first day of school, but right now it just feels right. I take the hollowed Bic from my book bag, load it, and stick my head out the window. "Look for me all you want," I shout.

Then I launch a wad that splatters right between his eyes.

I use my time on the plane to take one more look at the information packet that Dr. Carter mailed me. Keeping my head buried in my notes means I don't have to talk to the couple from Santa Barbara sitting in the middle and aisle seats. Still, I overhear more than I want. They've booked themselves a four-day Amazon cruise, and they're praying that the food will be edible and that the shipboard band will play songs they can dance to—"a dance that doesn't end in a vowel" is how the man puts it.

Certain facts from Dr. Carter's notes were common knowledge among the botany community. I mean, it's stuff you *have* to know—the vegetation in the Amazon Basin provides about one-third of the world's oxygen; the Amazon provides about one-fifth of the fresh water in the world; the Amazon is the second longest river in the world at 3,900 miles; there are over 18,000 plant species in the basin. I already knew that the extremely heavy rainfall robs the soil of its nutrients and makes real farming impossible.

The long flight reduces my normal level of pickiness about my reading material. Poring over the tourist-oriented booklets the airline has stuck in pouches behind the seats, I absorb all kinds of Brazilian trivia. It seems that the majority of the Indians in the Amazon Basin are dark-skinned and of unknown descent, and there are plenty of theories about that. Some say, based on their resemblance to the tall Polynesians, that they drifted over the Andes from Peru about the same time that other Peruvian Indians were taking boats for the South Seas. Others say these natives always lived in the heart of the jungle and that it's just the harsh light of science flushing them out. More people than you'd imagine believe their ancestors were survivors of the lost continent of Atlantis. There are supposed to be 170 tribes left, each with its own language and religion, but like the native population of North America, they've been continuously pushed off their land and they've fallen victim to diseases brought in by outsiders. The best estimates suggest that there were between 2 and 5 million Indians living in the land that makes up modern Brazil when the Portuguese first arrived in 1500. Now there are around 200,000 total.

The Santa Barbara woman leans across me, blocking my light. We've been flying all night, and for the first time, there's sunlight outside the window.

"Ken, look at that," she says, nudging her tanned husband.

I look down, myself, but at first I don't

understand what she's talking about. We must still be over the ocean. But as I focus, I see that it's not the ocean. It's too green, but it goes on forever, or at least as far as I can see. Then I notice a blue ribbon cutting through the green. What I'm really looking at—and my heart races at this realization—is the Amazon. I remember something from the notes, and I flip back through the pages. It says the Amazon region accounts for 60 percent of Brazil's total territory. It covers an area greater than all of Western Europe. Staring out the window, a shiver runs up my spine.

An hour and a half later, we're on the ground in Belém, Brazil. The plane stops in the middle of the runway. There's no motorized ramp connecting the plane to a terminal—just a creaky and dented stair-ramp that they roll up to the door. I don't have to wait long for my bag once I've deplaned. They just hand it to me right there. I managed to get all my stuff except for my laptop into a giant backpack. I have trouble keeping my balance as I swing the thing up around my shoulders. I teeter on one leg for a second, praying I don't embarrass myself by letting the weight of the bag topple me completely over. I'm a good hundred yards from the terminal and as I walk toward it in a stream of other travelers, I'm wondering what I'll do if whomever is supposed to pick me up isn't there. I'm curious about how they're going to spot me. I hadn't sent anyone a picture, but then again, how many thirteen-year-olds are getting off a plane in the Amazon by themselves?

I shouldn't have worried. As I push through the double glass doors, I spot a scruffy, glasses-wearing guy holding up a cardboard sign with GRADY JACOBS scrawled across it in green Magic Marker. The lanky man looks to be in his mid-twenties and has the same sort of weary look as the grad students Dad's brought home for dinner. The guy looks right through me, though I'm walking straight at him. Even when I'm standing three feet in front of him, he keeps looking over my shoulder toward the double doors.

"I'm Grady," I say.

He glances down at me, but only briefly. "I'm looking for Grady Jacobs, kid," he says. He's not exactly unfriendly, just a bit put out by my disturbing him.

"That's me," I say, reaching into my pocket for my passport. "Did you need to see some ID?"

"Grady Jacobs, the UCLA freshman? Winner of the past two National Science Fairs?" he asks. He looks concerned. "There isn't a limo waiting outside, in case this is some kind of joke."

"Grady Jacobs—freshman at Woodrow Wilson High School. National Science Fair grand champion," I respond. I hold up my passport photo.

"My oh my," the man says, starting to laugh. "Wait until Dr. Carter gets a load of you."

My escort's name is Roddy. He's been working for Dr. Carter for ten months, which means he has the least seniority of the five in the group. That's why he got the lackey job of picking me up. He explains this on a cab ride to the docks on the edge of the river. On the drive I keep my face pressed to the dirty glass of the back window, watching the ocean of people flow back together as we pass. The range of skin tones amazes me. I live in Los Angeles, which is supposed to be the ultimate melting pot of races, but it can't hold a candle to what I'm seeing in the streets and markets of Belém. Skin colors range from sunburned Nordic white, to bronze, to caramel, to lightly creamed coffee, to a black so deep, I swear it looks blue.

When we arrive at the docks, Roddy hands the driver a few coins as he gets out of the car. I follow him from ragtag boat to ragtag boat. At each he speaks in Portuguese to whatever crew member is available. His words come out too quickly for me to understand many of them. The sixth boat we get to is full of bottles of rum; sacks of flour, sugar, and coffee; and goats. Roddy breaks into his familiar chatter, and the next thing I know, he's hopping onboard.

"Come on, Grady. Your chariot awaits."

It takes me just four hours to lose my plane

food over the side of the boat. Roddy doesn't see me. He's sound asleep, sitting almost upright on a bench seat in the back. Just before sunset, we reach a section in the river so wide, I can't see either bank from the middle. When it gets dark, things get scary. I still haven't been able to look at food—not even the Snickers in my bag. The goats have crapped all over the deck. The crew has broken into the rum. They're shouting in a language I can't understand. If it weren't for the gas lantern hanging from the mast, I wouldn't be able to see a thing. I've never experienced dark like this. In Los Angeles, you can never see stars because the lights of the city don't allow the stars to shine through. Tonight I can see a million. Odd since I can barely see my fingers when I hold them up to my face.

A hand on my shoulder makes me jump out of my seat.

"Take it easy, Grady."

"Sorry," I say.

"This is for you," Roddy says, dropping something in my lap. It feels like nylon, like a giant basketball net.

"What is it?" I ask.

"A hammock."

And that's how I spend my first night on the Amazon: tied up between two posts, swinging gently in the breeze with the sound of rum-drunk sailors singing something that, because of all the laughter, I suspect is nasty. I fall asleep thinking how cool it would be if I had a parrot and an eye patch.

I feel better by morning, less nauseated. Roddy is already up, fishing. I've never tried the sport before. Dad isn't exactly the fishing type. I may have studied botany because I didn't want to hang out with people; Dad chose physics so he would rarely have to venture outdoors. Roddy hands me a pole and gives me some rudimentary instructions. Before long, I've caught my first catfish. Getting the two-pounder on board isn't so difficult, but I have no idea what to do next. He just flops around on deck. I don't know whether I should keep reeling it in or what. The dark-skinned sailors start laughing and pointing. I can see the hook sticking all the way through the silver fish's lower jaw. Its eyes seem to look up at me. Roddy places his tennis shoe on top of the fish's body, picks up a rum bottle, and cracks it down on the fish's head.

"Law of the jungle," he says, looking up at me and smiling. He picks up the body with his hand. "This next lesson you'll just get once. After that, you're on your own." He pulls a large folding knife out of a fanny pack and slices the fish down the belly, spilling its guts into the river. "Piranha food," he says.

A few cuts later, he hands me the filet. "Breakfast."

I cook the piece of fish on a gas-fueled hot plate.

After that, I survive the next thirty-six hours on fish and canned beans. The riverbanks, for the most part, are dense with 100- to 150-foot-tall trees. On the morning of the second day, we go several miles without seeing a tree. Instead, the land has been clear-cut for what I'd guess to be thousands of acres. More cows than I've ever seen in my life graze across the land that was once forest.

At the Hard Rock Cafe in Los Angeles, they have a billboard-sized digital signboard that gives a constant readout of the number of people alive on the planet and the number of acres of rain forest left in the world. The population spirals out of control upward while the acres of rain forest steadily diminish. The implication is, of course, that someday in the future, we'll have too little of the latter for the former to take simultaneous breaths.

Dr. Carter has been pretty secretive about the nature of the research we'll be doing down here. His e-mail refers to it as "a study of plant life that can only be conducted deep within the Amazon." I'm thinking that maybe it has something to do with deforestation. Roddy's sprawled motionless on the deck like a basking lizard. He's wearing sunglasses. I ask him what we're researching. I can't see his eyes, but my guess is that they're closed, and that he doesn't want to open them to answer my question.

"A study of plant life that can only be conducted deep within the Amazon," he says.

"Gee, thanks."

Just before sunset, the boat we're on pulls up to a makeshift dock. Indian children from a series of huts built along the banks of the river come running out to the boat. Roddy yaps at them in a friendly tone. I don't know what language he's speaking, but I'm fairly certain it's not Portuguese. He points to a stack of boxes and gas cans that have been pushed to the edge of the boat by the small crew. The children start grabbing boxes and gas cans, dragging them down the length of the dock.

"Here's where we get off," Roddy says.

A little boy tries to grab my laptop bag, but I hold on to it with a firm grip. Roddy says something and flips the boy a coin. The kid lets go and runs to catch up with the rest of the munchkin moving company. Roddy hands a few bills to the captain of the boat. At least I suppose it was the captain. He was the oldest, and he wore a cap—a souvenir item from a 1988 Janet Jackson tour.

Roddy and I follow the kids up what passes for a road—basically an eight-foot-wide path where the trees have been cut down. Waiting for us at the end of the road is a beat-up Toyota four-wheel-drive pickup. It's been jacked up to clear the stumps underneath, and the paint is worn nearly all the way off the sides from the sides of the vehicle getting scratched by the underbrush. By the time we catch up, the little kids have already expertly loaded the bed of the truck. Roddy takes out a handful of coins and divides them equally among the hands. Two of the kids try to get back in line after collecting their first share, but Roddy doesn't fall for it.

I have to use a stump as a step to climb all the way into the trunk. I notice that the keys have been left in the ignition. Roddy swings himself up into the cab and turns the key. The Toyota fights him for a minute before it turns over.

"Nearly there," Roddy says as he jams the transmission into first and starts us on the bumpy road to the campsite.

But "nearly there" means four hours of bouncing on the worn springs of the bench seat in the cab of the truck. It's well after midnight when Roddy flips on the CB radio and speaks into the microphone. "This is Roddy," he says. "Who's up?"

A woman's voice crackles out of the speaker a few seconds later.

"It's Sonja. You got Friday with you?"

"Affirmative," says Roddy, "but you might warn Dr. C that he's not . . . well, he's not—"

Sonja's voice cuts in. "He's not what?"

Roddy glances over at me. "Well, he's not as tall as we thought he'd be."

"You're losing it, Rod. How far out are you?"

"Half an hour. Get my pipe and slippers ready."

"I'll draw you a bath," she says, but I'm almost positive she's being sarcastic.

Roddy racks the microphone, but leaves the CB power on.

"Why did she call me Friday?" I ask.

Roddy smiles at me. "You ever read *Robinson Crusoe*?"

4

Sonja, a short, dark-haired, athletically built woman who appears to be about twenty-five, is the only one awake when Roddy and I finally arrive at camp. She takes one look at me, rolls her eyes, and says to Roddy, "Carter's going to have a cow." She doesn't say a word to me. I probably ought to be offended, but I'm too distracted by Sonja's looks. Her picture would fit right into a newspaper story about a fiery Romanian tennis star who shoots her playboy fiancé in a fit of jealousy. Sonja is gorgeous, but not in a Barbie doll way. Definitely more of an action figure. She's wearing a sleeveless orange T-shirt that reveals a tiny, unidentifiable tattoo on her well-defined bicep. I realize I'm gawking. So does Sonja; she rolls her eyes and walks into the adjacent room, shaking her head.

"Cow and a half," Roddy replies, raising his voice so she can hear him over the clattering electric fan she's turned on.

I guess *everyone* thought I was going to be older.

Roddy directs me to a tent and helps me tie

up my hammock in the dark. My eyes adjust well enough—aided by the light coming from the tent we've just exited—to see two other bodies already conked out. One of them I would have been able to *hear* regardless. He snores like a drunk troll.

"We'll worry about introductions in the morning," Roddy says as he climbs up into his own hammock. "And don't sweat the reception you're gonna get. Remember, they're scientists, which means they're not fully functional socially."

It occurs to me that the description fits me pretty well too. Doesn't matter either way. I'm used to people not liking me. I'm initially concerned about falling asleep over the snoring, but I blink, and the next thing I know, one of those old-fashioned windup clocks with the bells on top is clanging. I open an eye, see it's still dark, and pray the alarm was a mistake. But the other forms in the room are rolling out of their hammocks.

"Rise and shine, Gilligan," Roddy's voice emanates from the entrance flap. "Breakfast time."

Wiping sleep from my eyes, I trudge along behind the other three men. We return to the tent Roddy and I visited the night before. This time, though I may be sleepy, at least I'm not physically exhausted. I take a look around. This tent appears to serve the function of kitchen, communications center, and general meeting room. Gas-powered generators buzz quietly out-side the front door. A couple dim lamps illuminate the table, and a small red LED light on the cof-feemaker reveals that it's sucking up the juice as well. The men in front of me pour themselves cof-fee, pick up plates, and approach Roddy, who is busy frying something on a hot plate. I grab uten-sils off a two-by-four-and-plywood table and get in line. The mystery food turns out to be fish. I appraise it. I've eaten six meals in Brazil so far; five of them have included fish, the other a bag of vinegar-flavored potato chips and the Snickers I'd picked up at the airport.

"More fish?" I say to Roddy. I guess I sort of whine it. He flinches, then almost imperceptibly shakes his head "no," but it's too late. The other men have taken note of my existence.

"Maybe you'd like some pancakes and maple syrup," says the first man, older than Roddy, but not by much. Maybe thirty. Like everyone else I've seen in camp, he's muscled but lean. A little patch of facial hair clings to his lower lip. "Roddy, can we get his mom on the radio? Tell her to squeeze out some milk and overnight it down to him."

The other man, a long-haired Asian wearing a "Question Reality" T-shirt, takes a harder look at me. "I thought you were going to college. You look ten."

I don't really look ten. He's just baiting me.

"It's just that I've had fish for five meals in a—"

"Grady, meet Jack Springer and Francis Chen, both runners-up in our campwide Mr. Congeniality contest."

They grunt at me. I don't say anything else. I just take the fish from Roddy and eat in silence. I'm thirsty, but the only drink available is coffee, and I don't want to ask if there's anything else. I suffer. Minutes later, the flap to the tent is pulled back and Sonja enters with a small, wiry man, who I realize must be Dr. Carter. Apparently Sonja hasn't warned him, because his eyes narrow when he sees me. His head cocks to one side, and his eyebrows squeeze together. "Who . . . ," he says—his first word registers as a high note, and it's followed by a long pause before he completes his thought—"are you?"

"Grady Jacobs."

He looks at me like he can't fathom what I'm saying. I try to help. "The Embryo Project. Remember? You sent me a bunch of e-mails."

"I sent e-mail," he says, "to the reigning National Science Fair champion in botany who happened to have a UCLA e-mail destination. I assumed I would get a full-fledged adult, not someone we'd need to baby-sit."

"I have a UCLA e-mail address because my dad is a professor there," I answer, ignoring the insult.

"He doesn't like fish," says Jack Springer.

Dr. Carter ignores the comment. "So

Daddy's a professor at UCLA, and you just happened to win two National Science Fairs. Isn't that interesting?"

I don't like what he's implying. "My dad is a physics professor. He doesn't know much about botany."

"And I suppose you don't know any of the professors in the botany department at UCLA?"

"A couple," I say.

"Friends of your father?"

"Yeah, but—"

"And did they help you out?"

"Just setting up my greenhouse and getting some of the—"

"That's what I thought."

"Should we send him back?" asks Sonja. She says it like I'm not even here in the room with them.

Dr. Carter strokes his chin before shaking his head no. "We can use Roddy in the field, give the boy Roddy's duties, and see if he can manage them. That Embryo funding will be useful. He'll sink or swim in the first week. If he sinks, we'll put him back on the plane."

"Roddy," Dr. Carter says, "train him today. I want you sapping by tomorrow. Is that clear?"

"Sir yes sir! As a bell, sir!" Roddy bellows, jerking his body into a bolt-upright position and saluting in imitation of a servile buck private. His wiseacre grin quickly disappears after a stern look from Dr. Carter.

Dr. Carter lifts the lid on a cardboard box and pulls out one of those bowl/boxes of cereal. I can't read the Portuguese name on the box, but the picture of Tony the Tiger makes translation unnecessary. From a generator-powered refrigerator he grabs a jug of milk. Dr. Carter sits down across from me and pours the milk on the cereal. I pull a fish bone from my mouth, and Carter reaches across the table and grabs my elbow. He shakes my arm, and my soft flesh jiggles like Jell-O.

Carter shakes his head. "Don't get too excited, Roddy. You'll probably be back taking care of base camp within the week."

Dr. Carter, Sonja, Jack, and Francis load themselves down with equipment and are gone by dawn. Roddy says to watch closely, but what he's doing hardly requires note-taking. First he gathers all the metal dishes from the breakfast table and loads them in a mesh sack. "Follow me," he says, slinging the bag over his shoulder.

I see the camp for the first time in daylight. It's set up in a small clearing in a river basin. The river's about thirty feet wide, fast-moving, and not very deep. Five military green tents arranged within a fifty-foot radius remind me of the ones in *M*A*S*H*. Roddy lists their functions for me. Three of the tents serve as quarters for Dr. Carter and the researchers. One is the meeting room/kitchen I'd already seen. The final, largest one is the lab. It's slightly different

ROB THOMAS

from the others: Planks have been laid across a foundation of logs so that it sits about two feet off the ground. The other tents have plywood floors set directly on the ground. Someone has also gone to the trouble of building a real thatched roof with palm leaves over the tent. There are two power generators outside the lab, as opposed to one outside the kitchen. Elsewhere, there's a total lack of power.

Roddy and I scrub pans with steel wool on the bank of the small river—he says the team calls it the 'Zonlet.

"So this is my chance of a lifetime to do research in the Amazon?" I say to Roddy.

"You gotta start somewhere," he says.

The rest of the day doesn't get much better. After doing dishes, we bury trash. Then we go out and check fishing lines along the 'Zonlet, throwing the catches in a sack and rebaiting hooks. The trails along the stream are often steep, and it seems like I have to constantly duck under vines or climb over logs. When we return, we gut and clean the fish. This process is still taking some getting used to for me. Roddy cleans four fish in the time it takes me to finish my first one. These we throw in the small fridge. Already I'm exhausted. For lunch, Roddy pulls what looks like a giant fluffy tortilla out of a plastic sack and smears peanut butter from an industrial-sized can across it. He tears the bread in half and hands me one of the sections. We

46

drink sun tea. Afterward Roddy gets out a machete and snags a coconut from a pyramid that's been stacked outside the kitchen. I start to tell him I hate coconut, but I think better of it. Besides, I'm still hungry. I think I could choke down anything. Roddy hands me a section of the white meat, and I'm surprised to find the fruit doesn't taste anything like the flaky, dry stuff they ruin candy with back home. It's sweet, and has a consistency more like an apple. I devour it.

"Glad to see you like coconut," Roddy says enigmatically.

I learn why after lunch. It's Roddy's duty— soon to be mine—to collect the fruit.

"I didn't know they grew here," I say. "I thought coconut trees just grew wild on the coast."

"Missionaries," Roddy says. "They planted them in the jungle in this area. A few of the groves actually took off."

We end up having to hack our way through a weed-choked stretch of about fifty yards to find them. Roddy explains that the same path has been cleared and recleared countless times, never taking more than two weeks to regrow. After twenty or thirty minutes, my arm is so tired that I can barely lift the machete. The job only gets more difficult. Roddy teaches me how, using a sixty-inch belt of leather, to climb the tall trees and hack down the coconuts. The height would terrify me, if I weren't so focused on my fatigue. When we get back to camp, Roddy leads me back into the kitchen. He takes a huge pot down from a rack and asks me to go fill it with water.

"What for?" I ask.

"Look," says Roddy, "let me give you some advice. You can ask me all the questions you want, but Dr. Carter and the rest of them consider it an honor for you—for me, even—to be out here. You're going to be able to include this study on your résumé, and that'll be valuable to you for the rest of your life. So listen to what I'm saying: Just do as they tell you."

I walk toward the flap with the pot in my hand.

"By the way. It's for rice," says Roddy.

"So that's all I'm going to be here? A cook and a maid?"

Roddy smiles at me. "Smile, Friday, there's a bit of science thrown in. Your day is far from over."

The others return to camp just as it begins to get dark. After dinner—rice, that strange flatbread, and canned chili—Roddy and I clean the dishes, then make sack lunches for the next day and throw them in the fridge. All I want to do now is sleep. Every muscle in my body aches. I can hardly pay attention as Roddy shows me how to work the coffeemaker and where all the stuff for breakfast is. Tomorrow the duty is mine.

"All right," he says, putting his fists on his

hips, "time to put on your scientist cap."

He leads me out of the kitchen tent and over to the lab. It's my first time to actually go in, and I'm impressed by what I see. Other than a lack of running water, it's well equipped. There's one desktop computer: an awesome custom-built Sun Microsystems workstation with massively parallel processors and RAID storage banks, satellite uplink to the Internet, 1200-dpi color laser imagers, and Hell drum scanners. The lab has a portable JEOL JSM 840A scanning electron microscope, spectroscopes, full capability for DNA analysis, self-sterilizing specimen-prep area, autoclave, critical point dryer, vacuum evaporator . . . you name it!

Despite all the high-tech gear on hand, everyone seemed to be working on humble laptops. I follow Roddy around. He collects the samples each scientist has gathered, inserts them in Ziploc Bags, and labels them according to the instructions he's been given. One by one, the group finishes typing their findings into their computers. They save these both on their internal hard drives and Jaz drive cartridges. The cartridges are handed to Roddy. As soon as Dr. Carter gets up from the main computer, Roddy sits down and inserts the first disk. Over the next sixty minutes, I'm taught what Roddy calls the most critical job I'll do. From each cartridge, he takes the findings of the individual scientists and plugs them into the overall group project.

Then he updates a series of pie charts and bar graphs. By now we're alone in the lab, and the others have gone to bed. I realize that what he's doing—what I'll be doing—is no more than what my mother is doing for me back home. Recording data. As a matter of fact, it's less than what Mom's doing. I'm not even conducting any of the measurements or evaluations. I'm just transferring the findings from individual sources to a combined database. Couldn't they have just trained a chimp?

"So what is the overall goal of the project?" I ask Roddy as he prints a document labeled GROWTH RATE 3-2. "As chief caterer, I demand to know!"

"What have they told you?" he asks as he pulls a series of documents from the laser printer and begins to collate them.

"Not much. I'm guessing it has something to do with deforestation."

"Yeah, that's part of it. We're funded by the Brazilian government, the United Nations, the Sierra Club, and the beef industry."

"Strange bedfellows," I say.

Roddy shakes his head. "You're a weird thirteen-year-old, Grady."

"That's what people tell me."

"Anyway," Roddy continues, "the reason for these 'strange bedfellows' is that everyone wants an independent study done. A study commissioned by the beef industry wouldn't be worth the paper it was printed on. Neither would a Sierra Club–funded study."

"So, they commission one of the most respected botanists in the world, and everyone with an interest in the results chips in."

"That keeps it clean. Our recommendation is going to have a huge impact on what the Brazilian government does in the Amazon."

For a minute I consider what he's said, but something doesn't quite make sense to me. "Isn't it just a matter of adding up what you gain and what you lose through deforestation? It doesn't seem like they'd need this team for that."

"Yeah, but it's not that simple. We're not just adding up what's lost and what's gained. We know that no matter what we report, we're not going to halt deforestation, so what Dr. Carter has been working on for the past three years are 'super trees'—trees that grow more quickly than other trees, have double the carbon dioxide uptake rate, produce twice as much oxygen . . ."

"So that half the forest could produce the same amount of oxygen and provide millions of acres for ranching. Everyone wins."

"Exactamundo."

"What about the rest of the ecosystem? The animals? The people?"

"Well, that's part of what they're studying."

Roddy staples six packets of information together. Then we go around and hook up all the laptop batteries to chargers, switch off the computers, and turn off the lights. Before we head back to bed though, we stop in the kitchen and spread the packets out so they'll be available for everyone at breakfast. For the research team, these graphs and charts take the place of a morning paper.

I start to follow Roddy out of the tent, but he stops me. "Whoa there, little buddy."

"Yeah, Skipper?"

"You're going to want to bed down in here. Trust me. It'll give you a couple extra minutes of sleep. This way your alarm clock won't wake up the professors and Ginger. A well-rested castaway is a happy castaway, and a happy castaway is one who doesn't send you back to America."

Roddy pulls a folding cot from behind a stack of boxes. "You go ahead and get ready for bed. I'll run over to the other tent and bring you my old alarm clock."

I don't remember seeing Roddy again. I remember taking off my shoes. I remember lying back on the cot. That's it. Then I'm dreaming: I'm having dinner; we've ordered pizza; I've got an ice-cold Coke; Mom's dishing up ice cream; I'm taking a bath; I'm lying down in my queen-sized water bed.

The alarm goes off. I would swear I haven't slept at all, except that it's a glow-in-the-dark clock face, and it reads 5:15 A.M. I reach above me, grab the device, and search for a "snooze" button in the dark. I can't get the thing to shut off, and every muscle in my body is screaming at me. I'm so incredibly sore. Finally I struggle out of bed, flip on a light, and take a good look at it. The stem of the alarm lever has been broken off. From the precision of the cut, I'd say it was intentional. I have to use a toothpick from the table to poke inside the clock and get the lever flipped to the off position.

Okay, so I'm awake. I've had my five hours of sleep. Just what every growing boy needs.

On the plywood table I see a note from Roddy. It's a things-to-do list. The first several are in reference to breakfast. I start the coffee, measuring everything out like Roddy showed me. I take out a match and get the hot plate fired up. I put on my shoes and limp out to fill the generators with gas, and a tub with water from the stream. I come back and begin to melt a little bit of butter in the pan. I pull out a cereal box with Toucan Sam on the cover and crunch greedily through a bowl of Fruit Loops. I throw the first fish fillets in the frying pan and listen to them sizzle. Then I wander from tent to tent, poking my head in and shouting, "Rise and shine. We're burning daylight here."

I'm silent throughout breakfast. The only two words said to me during the meal are from Jack. "Coffee's weak," he says. I make a mental note to add another teaspoon of Folgers.

The rest of my day is spent checking off items from Roddy's list. Most of it is a repeat of what we did yesterday, except that instead of chopping down coconuts, he has me gather tangerines. He's drawn a little map on the paper, and fortunately they're not far from the coconut trees, so I'm able to use a good part of the trail we cut through yesterday. I count one tarantula, three parrots, and some kind of strange-looking opossum as I'm wandering through the jungle.

After making myself lunch—tangerines, flatbread, and canned cocktail weenies—I take out my laptop. Before I left L.A., I had a cellular modem installed per Dr. Carter's instructions. There aren't exactly phone lines available in the middle of the Amazon. I dial up the server. The modem shrieks, and the menubar lets me know I'm connected. I have four pieces of mail, and they're all from Mom. I open the most recent.

Grady,
You are scaring us to death, son. I cannot believe we still haven't heard from you since you've been gone. Your father has called Embryo trying to get in touch with you by radio. (I assume there's one at the site.) So far he's had no luck. If we don't hear from you within the week, you can bet that we'll be down there looking for you. I told you to call me from the airport to let me know you were picked up. Don't forget you're only thirteen years old. I was crazy for letting you go.

GREEN THUMB

Let me know how you're being treated. Are
you having fun there? Learning a lot? Are
you eating okay? If you're not lost or
suffering from some mysterious jungle disease, I hope you're having a good time.
Incidentally, two boys came by the house
looking for you. They said they were
friends of yours. I knew you were making
friends, young man. I told them they
should come spend the night once you get
back from Brazil. They said they'd like
that. Is it the current fashion for boys
to shave their heads? I'm happy that you
haven't decided to do that.
Write or call now!
Mom
P.S. The enclosed file contains all the
updated data for the greenhouse project.

I download the file before banging out a
return message.

Mom,
Call off the cavalry. I'm fine.
Everything's great here. I'm learning a
lot about how research teams work. I'm
getting plenty of protein in my diet.
Don't worry,
Grady

The next three weeks pass slowly. At the end
of each of the first two, Dr. Carter tells the others, "We'll give him one more week." He hasn't
said a thing about me since, so I think I may be
here for the duration.

Dr. Carter is, like my father, a scientist, but
everything else about him is dissimilar. First of
all, the man is tiny. *I* may even outweigh him.
Plus, I'm probably an inch or two taller, which
would make him about five three. While my

father is shaped sort of like a snowman, Dr. Carter might be more readily compared to a scarecrow. Like most scientists I've met, Dad doesn't spend much time fixated on appearances. His hair, though washed regularly, is usually a mop of curls in desperate need of a trim. Dr. Carter's short, straight hair is gelled and parted in such a precise manner that I swear he must use a surveyor's scope to plot its course. Whereas Dad's features are pronounced—golf ball eyes, sweet-potato nose, the mouth of a halibut—Dr. Carter's seem so small as to hardly exist, like a cartoon with dots and lines instead of body parts. It's difficult to explain in terms beyond the physical, but *everything* about my dad—except his brain—is loose and soft, and everything about Dr. Carter—including his brain—is rigid and rock hard. Dad believes a well-rested brain is a productive brain. He's got a big couch in his office, where I've often found him snoring in the middle of the afternoon. No one in Dr. Carter's crew sleeps more than six hours a night. (I sleep an hour and a half less, though I've gotten my duties down to the point that I can sometimes sneak in an hour or two nap in the afternoon.) In Dad's lab, a democracy exists. His grad student assistants and junior professors all have different ideas about the right way to find a solution to a problem. Dad listens to their suggestions, considers them, and sometimes—even when he thinks his way is the right way—lets someone else take charge, because he thinks it's good for morale. Dr. Carter isn't like that. We do things according to his plan. I learned that quickly.

It was late at night during my second week after the team was back in the lab. I was wandering through collecting samples. Roddy, still the only person there who would occasionally speak to me beyond a "get me this" or "don't touch that," sat at his workstation peering through a microscope. He called me over and handed me two vials and gave me what sounded like normal instructions. "Label these 'Sap: normal tree, estimated age 150 years,' and 'Sap: super tree, age 3 years.'"

But at the same time Roddy gave me these instructions, Dr. Carter was walking by. The man nearly blew a gasket as he screamed at poor Roddy. "Who told you to collect samples from the new forest?" he shouted.

The other scientists stopped what they were doing to stare. Roddy looked like he wanted to slink away and die. "No one," he stammered. "I just thought it might be a good idea to compare—"

"If you don't want to go back to doing Grady's job, you'll just do what you're told around here. There were fifty applicants for your position who were just as qualified. Now you *can* be replaced. Grady could probably even manage limiting the sapping to the trees he was told."

I couldn't believe how Dr. Carter totally lost

it. Veins were bulging in his neck as he pushed his face up next to Roddy's. I'm sure Roddy was experiencing some saliva fallout. It almost looked like Dr. Carter wanted to hit the guy. Roddy sort of stood there with his head down, afraid to look him in the eye. The standard reaction to a bully. I hated watching it. It's the sort of thing I think bullies live for.

I was still standing there holding the two samples in my hand. Dr. Carter noticed me. "Bury those," he ordered.

I slipped them into my pocket figuring I would complete the task in the morning when I did the rest of the garbage. Dr. Carter stared at me like I'd grown a propeller on the top of my head. "Now!" he screamed.

I was too scared to wander out to where we bury garbage normally. I didn't like to venture that far from camp in the dark, so I got the shovel and dug a hole in the soft dirt on the bank of the 'Zonlet. As I was patting down the dirt with the back of the shovel, I heard a crack and I knew I'd broken the vial. For no reason other than conditioning, I cowered. I held my breath, relieved that no one had heard. Dr. Carter hated sample spills.

Lately I just try to stay away from Dr. Carter. I've been here nearly a month. At first, I thought that the summer was going to be a total waste—after all, I'm more servant than scientist—but I'm starting to take advantage of my situation.

GREEN THUMB

It's funny, but even though I'm a botanist, and plants naturally grow outdoors, it's occurred to me that this is the first time I've really seen plants in their natural habitat. Before, I've only seen them in labs and dealt with them as isolated units. Now I'm observing how they exist as part of the ecosystem. I've started to keep my own samples. I've snuck a handful of Ziploc Bags out of the lab, and every day I'm clipping two or three varieties of plants I've never seen, not even in textbooks; and I store them underneath the thin mat of my cot. I've also started keeping a journal on my laptop.

A couple days ago, I saw my first tropical orchid. It was growing out of a raised root of a tree growing alongside the 'Zonlet. The amazing thing to me was that my first thought was that it was the most beautiful thing I'd ever seen— not that I was seeing a rare and extremely valuable *Odontoglossum crispum*. I didn't even take a clipping from it, but as I was bending over the flower I noticed something behind it so unfamiliar that it caused me do a double take.

The unfamiliar thing was me, or rather my reflection, in the water. The heat and humidity of life near the equator meant that I usually had my T-shirt off by midmorning. I'd tie it around my waist and just put it on if I had to hack my way through thick underbrush that could rip at my body. The thing that struck me as so odd about my reflection was that it looked like it belonged to somebody else. The layer of baby fat that had seemed so much like a permanent cocoon was gone. Most of my shorts are the kind with elastic bands, and I'd noticed that they'd seemed a bit baggier, but I hadn't given it much thought. Looking at my reflection, I saw why. Instead of seeing the usual pear shape of my body, I observed how my shoulders actually tapered down diagonally to my waist. My stomach had flattened out, and I could make out the faintest of shadows of where pectorals might actually go. I was stunned to learn I had cheekbones. The biggest difference, though, might have actually been in my arms. All the climbing and hacking I'd been doing had resulted in defined biceps and triceps. I flexed in front of the stream and watched, transfixed, as muscles popped and rolled like living creatures under my skin.

As I stood there posing, I heard giggling coming from behind me. From the timbre of the laughter, I knew before I spun around that it came from a girl.

She looked to be about my age, and she was flanked on either side by smiling males a few years older. Indians—all three of them. The two men were carrying bows, and one of them had a small deerlike creature slung over his shoulder. The other had a bulging sack over his. They were wearing even less clothing than me. The men had belts of cloth tied around their waists with some sort of leather piece that covered all the important stuff. The girl was wearing what looked like a kimono cut off about midthigh. All three of them were tall—the men a bit over six feet and the girl an inch or two taller than me. I was reminded of a theory I read on the plane—one about the Indians of the Amazon being related to Polynesians.

I stood there gaping with no idea what to say. *Besides,* I thought, *what good is it going to do?* I could ask for directions and order a club sandwich in Portuguese, but I didn't speak a word of any of the Indian languages. Still, the moment was awkward, and I felt like I needed to speak. I said the only thing that seemed appropriate at the moment. "I am Tarzan, lord of the jungle."

The two men stared at me uncomprehendingly, but the girl opened her mouth and spoke in English. "Long way from Africa, aren't you?"

They stay for dinner. I learn that they're Urah-wau Indians who live in a village just up the 'Zonlet a few kilometers from our base camp and that they frequently serve as guides for the scientists. They also bring in the flatbread. Roddy explains how the Indians cut open buruti tree—one of the palms that seem to be everywhere—then grind up the core into a flour used to make the bread.

"Did we trade them a couple T-shirts for all this?" I ask.

"They give us this bread because they know we're here to help them. They see the forest shrinking, and they wonder when they'll be driven off their land."

The girl's name sounded to me like Su-kay-WAY-cha, but all the scientists just call her Sue. I serve dinner, though one of the Indian men actually prepares the meat. I have trouble keeping my eyes off Sue. She looks nothing like all the blond bulimic cheerleader-types roaming the halls of Northshores, but she's twice as beautiful. On top of being tall, she's sculpted like an Olympic swimmer. Her skin is the color and texture of hand-rubbed hardwood. Her black hair is straight and long, and when she walks it's as if she's perfected a motion that the rest of us have practiced for a lifetime without quite getting the hang of it. Hers is a silent and effortless glide.

Roddy helps me with the extra dishes after we've eaten.

"How did she learn English?" I ask.

He tells me the story as we walk down to the 'Zonlet with buckets. He's only heard the details secondhand from Sonja, but what he knows is that Sue was orphaned at three—her father killed in a raid by the warlike Kel-Ha-Nitika tribe in retribution for hunting on land too close to their village. Her mother was stolen. Not long afterward, a white couple—the Mormon missionaries who planted all the coconut trees—visited the tribe. They convinced the elders to let them raise the baby, promising they would teach her how to read and write and that someday she would be a great leader for the tribe, capable of dealing with the outside world on its own terms. Sue lived with the couple in a makeshift mission right on the Amazon for nine years. Though she loved them like parents, when they decided to return to America, Sue went back to the tribe. She's been a key voice in the tribe's decision to assist The Wood Stock Project. She's sure that, like the majority of scientists who have visited the Amazon, the group will issue a report cautioning against rampant destruction of the rain forest.

After Roddy and I finish cleaning up, it's time for the team to retreat to the lab. Sue and her two silent companions wave good-bye, and I watch as they turn and disappear into the jungle.

It's the fourth night in a row that I've looked at Francis's results and thought there was something wrong. Well, not exactly wrong, but that he's ignoring something. Francis is working with the sounds of the forest, using high-powered microphones to record samples from the "New Forest"—the area in which The Wood Stock Project has planted its super trees—and he's comparing the audio vibrations to those in the rest of the forest. The reasoning behind the experiment is simple. It's not always easy to "see" an ecological system returning to an area, but it's much easier to "hear" it. The sounds of jungle birds, insects, and animals can all be reduced to a specific pitch or frequency. By comparing the sounds—represented by lines on seismiclike readouts rather than actual sounds—of the old forest to the new, they can determine whether ecosystems are flourishing in the new areas.

I've looked at the charts for so long now that I recognize the distinctive zig of a monkey screaming, the gentle bumps of nighttime insects sawing their legs together, even the barely registering signal of vampire bats emitting their superhigh sonic radar. *Two* things bother me, actually. The first, I'm sure, disturbs everyone. The New Forest isn't producing any results. There are no "sounds of the forest." The audible vibrations that are picked up are so faint that they're probably from the old forest surrounding the new one. It's possible that some mammals aren't returning to the area just because of the humans working there every day. Then again, I see animals around our camp all the time.

The second thing that's bothering me is a little more vague. It's something that Francis is simply ignoring. Down at the bottom of the chart, in the area where the subtlest vibrations register—bats, sometimes—I can make out the smallest bumps in the graphs. Francis hasn't labeled these, he's just let them slide. At first I wasn't really sure I was seeing them correctly, but I used the magnification on the computer screen, and they're just too strange to ignore. They look almost like binary computer code, and the repetition of the frequencies suggest that it's a deliberately created sound.

If I didn't know better, I'd swear it was a language.

The next morning I catch Francis by himself before he sets off for the New Forest. I'm thinking that it's important that I speak my piece far from the others, as I doubt a thirty-year-old doctoral student is going to want someone who hasn't been to high school yet critiquing his work in front of his peers. I've printed out enlargements of the vibrations I've noticed and, as I speak, I try to maintain a deferential tone. "Hey, uh, Francis, can I have you take a look at something?"

He glances at his watch before responding. "What is it?"

I hold up the readouts and point to the vibrations that concern me. "You're not labeling these sounds that are registering at the highest frequencies, and I was . . . uh . . . just sort of wondering . . . uh . . . why."

Francis smirks. "*You* want to know why?"

"Well, I'm just curious. You label everything else, and I think you can tell by these patterns that whatever is making these sounds—"

Francis's laughter cuts me off. "Look Science Fair, this isn't Mr. Wizard's chemistry set you're playing with now. These vibrations you're seeing? I've isolated them already. They come from the trees—wind whistling through the leaves more than likely. I don't mark them because they mean nothing. I'm charting the biologicals. Nothing else. Now I appreciate the fact that you think you're smarter than everyone here, but instead of sticking your nose in where it doesn't belong, and where it's not qualified to be, why don't you get those dishes done."

I keep my mouth shut as Francis, shaking his head, turns and heads for his tent. It takes a lot of willpower for me to remain silent, because I know he's wrong. If he really thinks trees are making these perfectly regular and repeating patterns on the charts, then he'll probably think it'll be normal if the rain forest beetles break into a version of "Gangsta's Paradise."

By working up a real sweat, I'm able to complete all my brainless duties by early in the afternoon. After that, I make a decision that I know fully well could get me sent home. Entering the lab, I open the metal equipment closet and pull out the case that houses the backup microphone. It takes me a while, but I read the instruction manual, download the SoundZRight software on my laptop, plug the microphone into the appropriate port, and set it up in the middle of camp with the microphone pointed right at some of the tallest trees surrounding us. At first the bars and lines all jump up and down. The forest never seems silent to me, but by the looks of the readout, you'd think there was a rock concert taking place. Pecking away at the keyboard, I isolate the sounds that are registering and eliminate all frequencies other than the one I'm interested in. Once I've locked on to the correct one, I magnify it so that all I'm looking at on my monitor is the digital readout sliding across the screen. It's a clearer picture than Francis's jumbled graphs. It still shows me patterns that I think must be intentional. There's too much rhyme and reason to them to support any other hypothesis. Because the frequency registers in the same general area of the bats, my first thought is that maybe what I've locked on to is a species of bats. Lord knows they're plentiful around here: sword-nosed, long-tongued, vampire. You can't walk around at night without occasionally feeling their nasty wings flap against your arms.

Then I notice something that makes me think I'm an idiot. As I see the leaves move on the trees and I feel a breeze, the patterns on the graph change slightly. Maybe Francis is right. Maybe the phenomenon can be explained away as simply as that. The microphone is simply picking up a slight whistle as the wind cuts across the bark and the leaves of the trees. So why is it regular? Why do the lines on the graph form perfectly cut patterns in the chart instead of the random and haphazard ones I would expect from wind noise?

As I'm trying to work this out in my head, a coconut falls from one of the trees in front of me. On the monitor of my keyboard, the readout shows a distinctive change. I isolate it with the trackpad, cut it, and save it. I would never tell anyone what I'm thinking now. I'd get locked in a loony bin. I attempt an experiment just to eliminate this crazy notion swimming around in my head. I run inside the lab and unplug the battery-powered speakers from the desktop computer. Within a few minutes I have them hooked up to my laptop and pointed at the coconut tree. I'm glad my dad isn't here to watch this. What I'm testing has as much scientific logic behind it as Mom asking her philodendron which dress she should wear.

"Here goes nothing," I say as I call up the recorded bit that I've just saved.

I scroll down from the file menu, releasing the cursor on the "Play" command. It blinks. I don't hear a sound, but then, I wasn't expecting to. The frequency is out of my range of hearing. It doesn't matter. What I see is the important thing. And the thing I see is too outrageous for me to believe.

A coconut falls to the forest floor.

I walk the ten yards or so to where the coconut has come to rest. I take a look at it. It isn't ripe yet. There's no reason it should have fallen. Up in the tree, I notice there's one coconut left. I return to my computer and repeat the experiment.

The final coconut drops, hits the base of the tree, and keeps rolling until I stop it with my foot.

5

My experiments continue each afternoon. I fight my ego-driven desire to put on a coconut-harvesting demonstration for the other five members of The Wood Stock Project. I'd probably get sent home for having an independent thought—one unsanctioned by Dr. Carter. Who am I kidding anyway? I'm not a member of the team. I'm cheap labor. If they didn't bounce me for not following orders, they would surely get me for using equipment I'm not allowed to touch. In the week since the initial discovery, I've retested on another coconut tree—six for six. I've got a giant pyramid of the fruit built in front of the kitchen tent. Lately I've been isolating odd patches in the graphed readout, cutting these sequences and replaying them, then observing the motion of the forest. So far, using this method, I've figured out how to make trees "let go" of vines, how to make branches bend hard. And spookiest of all: When I wait until there's absolutely no wind before hitting "Play," the leaves rustle on their own.

I've made charts of all the sequences. They

seem to be comparable to binary computer code or Morse code—two different pitches that, when used in a certain order, send a signal. At first, the existence of a tree language made me consider the possibility that there was some sort of "brain" or nerve center that scientists had never discovered, but the more I study it, the further I get away from that theory. Instead, I'm beginning to relate what I'm seeing to human reflexes. The trees don't "consider" their actions like we consider whether we want to go to the store or whatever. It's closer to what happens when a doctor hits us in the knee with a rubber mallet and our foot kicks out. But instead of a humanlike relay of neurons, hormones, and DNA carrying nerve signals to the spine and back, a tree's primitive sensory receptors respond to stimuli as directly as a light to a switch. During the fall, deciduous trees like oaks drop their leaves when the light starts changing. Who says different plant species can't be affected in a similar way by other basic stimuli? Like sound.

What this means is that, while I probably won't be able to swap stories with the trees of the rain forest, with adequate study I should be able to predict and create responses. I'm tempted to e-mail Mom back home to tell her she can burn my citrus clones. With this discovery, they might as well engrave my name on that third consecutive National Science Fair trophy. I should tell them to put in a call to Switzerland while they're at it. I'll be clearing space in my trophy case for that Nobel Prize and opening an unnumbered bank account.

Eight days after my first discovery, Dr. Carter announces at dinner that, starting tomorrow, he'll be gone for six days. He's traveling to Belém for a meeting with representatives of the groups that commissioned the rain forest study. "Grady will get bumped up to sapping. Roddy, you'll assist Sonja in measuring oxygen output in the New Forest," he says.

That's going to put my own experiment on hold, but I have to admit that the fact that Dr. Carter is trusting me to work on the project excites me. It means he must respect me. I don't claim to know much about psychology—I've read a couple books, but it's not really my bag. But isn't it funny how we tend to care so much about where we stand in the eyes of people who treat us badly? I'd like to think I'm beyond that, and usually I am. But there's no getting around it: My respect for Dr. Carter's mind makes me want his approval.

Dr. Carter continues. "Our backers are anxious to see our results. I think I can put them off for another six weeks by showing them these charts and the photographs, but we can't afford to lose a day. We're almost there. Let's not slack off now that we're in the homestretch."

No one told me that I'd still be responsible for breakfast, but I guess I should have seen it coming. As Dr. Carter handed me his disks last night, he made a point of requesting oatmeal, the food that takes me the longest to prepare. Apparently he was worried I was having delusions of grandeur.

Mom and Dad have always refused when teachers, administrators, or I have suggested that I'd be happier if I skipped a few grades. For the first time, their decision makes sense to me. Since Dr. Carter assigned me to the sapping last night, even Roddy seems to resent my age. I dropped a sample he handed me last night, and he snapped at me.

"Pull your head out."

He said it loud enough for everyone, including Dr. Carter, to hear.

Whatever floats his boat. Like I've said, I didn't become a botanist to make friends.

We leave camp as soon as I come back with the dishes. Even though I won't be sapping in the New Forest, I'll get to see it for the first time. Some of the results I've seen the others bring in just make it seem so impressive—every tree on forty acres biologically engineered by Dr. Carter. The hike is longer than I thought it would be, nearly ninety minutes. As we're hiking, I try to imagine what this journey would have done to me during my first days here, six weeks ago. I never could have made it. They were smart to leave me behind. I've already made up my mind that I'm always going to work in the field, never again get stuck in a lab or a greenhouse.

The farther away from our base camp we get, the more creatures I see in the forest. A screaming match between squirrel and spider monkeys breaks out above the spot where I've stopped to re-tie my hiking boot. Already this morning, I've seen my first three-toed sloth, this giant ferret-looking creature called a kinkajou, and a green toucan. Big herds of tapirs come down to drink from the shallow, sandy banks of the 'Zonlet. They're unnerving the first time you see them: big, ungainly, and very similar to pigs from the neck down but with these smooth, oddly expressive faces and shiny black snouts that look like hacked-off elephant trunks. Most impressive to me, though, are the countless variety of both arboreal specimens and herbaceous vegetation. I cut small samples from some of the strangest I see. If I stopped to take samples of everything I've never seen before, I'd never keep up with the group.

We've been going steadily uphill on the entire hike, but eventually we top the crest of a hill and I can see down into a valley. The view is startling. First of all, hundreds of acres below us appear as barren and lifeless as photos I've seen of the Mars landscape. Roddy told me weeks ago that the New Forest had been introduced to a section that had been clear-cut for farming— farming that was doomed by the uniformly low nutrient content of the rain forest—but his description didn't prepare me for the devastation below.

Then I see the New Forest.

It's like a forty-acre island of green in a sea of nothingness. The trees are a full thirty to fifty feet taller than their centenarian cousins that encircle both the New Forest and the wasteland, making the vista look vaguely doughnutlike. I can't believe it's only been three years since these seedlings were planted. It seems like you could almost watch them growing. Viewing it makes me wonder what Dr. Carter's worried about. All he has to do is bring out The Wood Stock Project trustees to the very spot where I'm standing and let them get a look at what he's done. They won't even glance at the mountains of paperwork we've been preparing. The results are right here. Bigger than life. Suddenly I know why these people are so willing to work for such a tyrant. The man's a genius.

"Are you coming?" Roddy shouts back at me.

The rest of the party is thirty yards down the trail. I jog to catch up. As we arrive at the outer ring of the jungle, Sonja stops and gives me last-second instructions. "Take samples from the healthiest trees and from trees in decline. Stay on the fringes of the old forest. I'll blow the siren when it's time to return to camp."

The others head into the New Forest, and I want desperately to follow, but I just nod. They don't have much patience for impatience. I break off from the group and head into the darkness of the jungle.

By lunch I've sapped four trees, collecting the sticky substance in small vials, and carving small WS's and sample numbers into the trees. I record their location, type, height, estimated age, and relative health in a special program that Roddy loaded on to my laptop last night.

I type notes one-handed into my computer while eating my flatbread-and-catfish sandwich with the other. Minutes pass. I spit out small fish bones as I'm entering the pertinent information regarding my final sapping. As I pause, I notice something strange. The monkeys are silent. In fact, the only birds I hear sound very far away. The jungle is usually a constant jumble of sounds. Suddenly they're either gone or distant. It occurs to me that what I'm hearing right now may somehow be related to the relatively "quiet" samples that Francis has pulled from the New Forest. I click open the SoundZRight program and begin hunting through my saved files so I can compare the visual representation to what I'm hearing now. Maybe there's a clue as to why . . .

Suddenly I feel a sharp pain in my shoulder and I think I must have been stung by one of the monster insects buzzing around the forest, but when I glance down I see something is actually sticking out of me. The object puzzles me: It looks sort of like an upside-down hors d'oeuvre.

A sharp toothpicklike shaft imbedded itself in my shoulder, protruding through some sort of rubbery morsel. I reach over with my opposite hand and pull it out, discovering that it's in at least a half inch farther than it looked. It looks worse than it hurts. As a matter-of-fact, nothing is hurting at all. I'm feeling strange. Dizzy.

Then I hear a sound. A snap. Like a twig breaking.

I look up toward where I've heard the sound, and I see an Indian thirty feet above me in a tree. He's balanced on a thin branch, and he's watching me. In his hand is a long, thin tube. I've seen a number of Indians this summer, all along the river, plus Sue and the other two Urah-wau from her tribe. None of them have looked like this guy. His eyes are almost invisible because of the four-inch-thick black-and-red band painted horizontally across his face from his forehead down to the bottom of his nose. His legs and his chest are bare. His arms are covered in tattoos.

"Hello," I say, knowing he won't understand the word but hoping he'll be able to garner from the tone that I'm harmless. I try to stand, but I'm getting dizzier and I just fall back onto my butt.

The Indian doesn't respond. He just watches me. Then I see him take something out of a pouch on his belt. I don't recognize what it is immediately, but when he inserts it into the tube he's carrying, everything makes sense. Forest Indians use blowguns to hunt and fish, dipping the darts in poison. This one has already shot me once. He intends to do it again.

I can't run. I can't shout. I can barely focus. I wonder if I'm going to die here. My laptop beeps, letting me know that I should change batteries soon.

It beeps.

I had almost forgotten about the tiny speaker built into the unit. I have all my preisolated tree commands assigned to function keys. I'm so dizzy and confused though that I can't remember which key does what. I punch F1. Nothing happens. I reluctantly stare up into the tree. The Indian is still there, perched and as confident as any monkey or parrot out on one of the branches. He brings the blowgun up to his lips. He aims.

I punch F2.

The branches of the big tree sway as if they've just been hit by a gale force wind. Had the Indian been expecting it, he might have been able to hang on, but he's using both hands to steady the blowgun for the kill shot. The unexpected jerk of the branch throws him off. He tries to grab lower branches as he plummets to the ground, but he's unable to keep a grip. One of the lowest boughs catches him just under the jaw. The sound is sickening—a scream cut off by the thud of flesh and teeth jammed together. The Indian falls to the jungle floor, landing on his back. I stare at the heap, wondering what I'm going to do if he's dead, wondering what I'll do if he isn't. It could be thirty seconds or twenty minutes that I keep a vigil. I'm not sure. I can't measure time, but the form doesn't move.

One clear thought manages to cut through the fog of my brain—*I have to get back to the others*.

I pull myself up despite the fact that my hands and feet have both gone numb. I have to sort of look at each limb and will it to function. It feels like it takes forever to get my computer into my backpack and sling it around my shoulders. I have no sense of equilibrium. As I stumble out of the forest, I sort of bounce back and forth between trees like a pinball, using the trunks as sidewalls to keep me standing. If this is what it's like to be drunk, I'm never drinking. It's terrifying. I'm halfway expecting a tomahawk to cleave the back of my skull. I know I'm delusional now. Old cowboy movies are replacing reality. Eventually sunlight cuts through the permanent dusk of the deep jungle.

I stumble out into the light. A stretch of three or four hundred yards of essentially lifeless prairie separate me from the towering oasis of the New Forest—from the team, the people who can save me. If there's an antidote, they'll know it. Normally I could cover this distance in a minute, but now it seems like my legs are completely numb. At first I'm able to stagger ten to fifteen yards at a time without falling. Then, when I can't climb to my feet anymore, I crawl. I've cut the distance I have to travel in half, but each passing minute reduces my chances of making it back.

The numbness that has made my legs nearly useless has attacked my arms. The paralysis moves steadily toward my shoulders, making crawling a hopeless pursuit. I collapse, then roll over onto my back. I stare up at the clouds that I never see anymore living in the depths of the jungle. My mother used to say she knew she had a special child, because when she used to take me to the park, as a preschooler, she'd point up at the sky and ask me what I saw in the clouds.

She'd say, "Doesn't that one look like a castle? And that one's an elephant. Come on, Grady, what do you see in the clouds?"

And I'd say, "Rain."

Now I look up in the clouds and see my mother. I see her talking to her ferns about how her play went. Explaining to them why Dad couldn't make it. Answering the phone. I see her face when someone tells her I won't be coming home from the Amazon, blaming herself for not standing up to Dad, not standing up to me.

I've always been thankful I got my father's brain. I might have been luckier to get some of my mother's goodness.

I don't want to die here. I begin to roll.

Fifty yards. Forty. Thirty . . .

I reach the edge of the New Forest. I can go no farther. The poison is starting to work on my insides. I feel like I'm having to remind the muscles in my chest to keep working, keep me breathing. I lie on my side. The trees above me are truly majestic. Disease free. Tall and perfect. Not a bad place to end up. Then I notice something that strikes me as both strange and eerily prophetic.

A toucan is perched on a fallen branch just a few feet from my head. His eyes are wide open, and he appears to be staring right back at me, but the eyes don't blink. In his beak is a large orange-and-black beetle, writhing furiously in an effort to free itself. With a sudden jerk the beetle pops loose, drops to the ground, and scuttles noisily away. The toucan, I realize, is stiff and dead.

I can keep my eyes open no longer.

Softness. It's been so long that I've experienced
the sensation, my first thought is that this must
be the afterlife. If that's true, then the afterlife
is also completely dark. But I can hear sounds.
Children. Laughter. Drums. Voices.

Indian voices.

I've been captured. They're probably slicing
potatoes and scallions into a huge pot. Dusting
off the recipe for white-boy stew. Either that or
they took one look at me and decided they'd
found a virgin to appease the gods.

My head throbs in sync with the drums—I'd
kill for a couple ibuprofen—but the most com-
pelling need I have is for water. My tongue doesn't
feel like my own body part; it has the alien texture of a piece of dried meat someone's forced
halfway down my throat. I have no saliva, yet
the blankets—no, wait, the fur that I'm lying
on—is damp with sweat. My entire body, as a
matter-of-fact, is sopping wet. Oh, great. And
I'm naked.

I struggle to stand. The pain in my head
nearly knocks me back down, but my shoulder

brushes against something—a pole. That means I'm in a hut. Using the thick piece of cane to keep my balance, I wipe my eyes. It feels like the grit of the entire Amazon is loosened. My eyes water, and I wipe them again with the back of my hands. Vision is restored. There *is* light, a circular glow right in front of me. A door.

Fearing there will be guards on the other side, I slide as quietly as I can across the dirt floor of the hut. I'm shivering with cold, which is odd since the Amazon never gets below eighty degrees at this time of year. As I reach the portal, I pull back the heavy blanket draped down over it creating a tiny aperture to peer through. No guard in sight. In front of me, maybe fifteen yards, is a huge fire. Fifty or more Indians of all ages surround it. Luckily, a barrel-sized bush shields the entrance to the hut. Draped across its branches I see what I need—my clothes.

I pull back the blanket and step out into the night, keeping the bush between me and the fire. I snatch down my underwear and khaki shorts and pull them on quickly. My "Botanists Do It in Broad Daylight" T-shirt is hanging from one of the uppermost shoots of the bush. I have to jump to try to reach it. On my first attempt I fail.

"Need some help, Tarzan?"

I spin. Sitting behind me on an old trunk is Sue. Next to her, looking vaguely witchlike, is an ancient, toothless woman.

"I got it," I mumble with my thick tongue, my tone maybe a bit too defensive.

I jump up toward the bush again. This time—unconcerned about how much noise I make—I'm successful. Wiggling my way into it, I'm conscious of the fact that Sue has now been present for two of the most embarrassing moments of my life.

The old woman yaps something unintelligible to me, which Sue seems to understand. Sue looks back at me. "You're thirsty," she says more than asks.

I nod and then look around at the unfamiliar huts and faces that surround the fire before speaking. "Where am I?"

It's the next morning before I get answers to any of my questions. The old woman practically pushes me back into bed, though not before letting me drain a pitcher of water that she's mixed some kind of powder into. By the time I awaken, my headache is gone. Sue enters with slabs of flatbread. I realize when I see it how hungry I am. Plowing through one of the megatortillas, I listen as Sue fills me in on how I got to the Urah-wau village.

It turns out that Roddy was the one who found me on the edge of the New Forest, struggling to breathe. No one had any idea what was wrong with me. The American scientists had never seen anything like it. Finally they decided

I had been bitten or stung by some sort of snake or insect. They used their first-aid kit, but I didn't get any better. After I was carried back to camp, I stayed unconscious for a full day. That's when Sue and a couple others delivered the flatbread. Sue suggested they take me with them. If anyone could fix me, Sue said, their medicine woman could. At first, the scientists resisted, but Dr. Carter returned from his trip early and gave his permission. After they'd brought me to the village, Sue and two of the tribe's best trackers returned to the spot where Roddy said he'd found me. Sue says she already had a suspicion about what had happened to me. They retraced my steps and found the spot where I'd been ambushed.

As she's talking, Sue removes something from a pouch. "Is this what struck you?" she asks, holding up a dart identical to the one I pulled from my arm. I nod.

"Tell me what he looked like," she said, making it sound like more of an order than I would have liked from a girl my age.

I described my attacker. She asked me a couple questions about the markings on his face and the tattoos on his arms.

"Why did he want to kill me?" I asked.

"He probably didn't care one way or the other whether you died. He's Kel-Ha-Nitika; he probably wanted to steal from you. White men are known to carry expensive equipment that can be sold at any outpost along the river. Darts dipped in the curare

84

will kill a fish or a small animal. It will slow a large animal. Afterward, the kill becomes simple. Sometimes the victim will"—she stops and mutters to herself in her native language, trying to remember the word—"go unconscious."

"He was going to shoot me twice," I say. "What would that have done?"

This news appears to surprise Sue. "White men frighten many in the forest. Many think they have special powers. He must have thought one dart wasn't enough."

"What would a second dart have done?"

Sue looks at me for a moment. "You would not awaken."

For a moment Sue says nothing else, then she reaches back into her pouch. "What we are curious about, then, is why the attacker was unsuccessful with his second dart. I think the first dart began its work right away. Did you have a weapon?"

"No," I say.

"Then how did you manage this?" She holds up the object that she's withdrawn from her pouch. For a moment, I can't figure out what it is. Then I realize—it's the final half inch of the Indian's tongue.

"I don't know," I say. "He just fell."

"A Kel-Ha-Nitika warrior just fell from the tree?" It's apparent by her tone of voice that she doesn't quite believe me.

"I don't remember it very well," I say. "I may have thrown a rock at him."

"Good shot," she says dubiously. "One good thing that comes out of this. Once you've survived the curare poison, it loses its power over you."

"I don't plan on getting shot at again," I say.

"Well, I can think of one enemy you have in the forest," Sue says, waving the tongue at me.

Sue leads me back to camp three days after I first left. We arrive in the afternoon. The scientists are all still out in the field.

I have dinner prepared by the time the team comes staggering home from the New Forest. While they've never seemed particularly fond of me, I thought that the combination of a hot meal waiting for them and seeing that I wasn't, in fact, dead, would elicit at least a couple of "glad to see yous" and maybe a slap on the back or two. On the contrary, my presence inspires flagrant antipathy from those returning to camp. Roddy, I suppose, doesn't look exactly angry. His expression is tough to read, but if I had to label it something, I'd call it sympathy.

Dr. Carter doesn't waste much time getting down to business. "Pack your bags tonight, Grady," he says as he fills his plate. "You're going home tomorrow."

"Why?" I ask.

I'm guessing this is a reaction to my near death, or that, perhaps, he's e-mailed my parents and they're insisting I return. In either case, I want to know. Dr. Carter exhales impatiently, almost as if he can't believe he's being troubled for an explanation. "For disobeying orders. For conducting experiments without permission. For unauthorized use of The Wood Stock Project equipment. If this were the military, Grady, you'd be court-martialed. The only thing we can do is send you home. There, perhaps, you and your father can win more science fair prizes."

He cuts off another piece of fish before continuing. "In any case, don't plan on ever using me as a reference, as I fear I would not be able to give you a recommendation. I've already notified Embryo of your termination and informed them that our association with the organization will not continue."

He takes another bite and chews impassively, oblivious to the fact that he's just cut out my heart and crushed it in front of me.

I set my alarm for three-thirty in the morning, though I don't really need to. I can't sleep. I lie in bed thinking of everything I need to do. I'm packed already. I was told my laptop would be returned in the morning. Apparently, it's the computer that gave me away. After getting shot with the dart, I didn't shut down the SoundZRight program. Once they'd brought me back to camp, Sonja took a look at the screen, thinking it might provide a clue as to what had happened to me. It wasn't difficult to figure out that I had been conducting my own experiments and that I had used the spare microphone. According to Roddy, there had been plenty of laughter earlier at the dinner table as Sonja told the others about what she'd seen.

"You wouldn't believe it," she said, "but it looked as though he was trying to uncover a secret plant language based on insignificant wind noise."

The three men guffawed. Of course, who am I to be offended? I laughed every time I caught my mom talking to the houseplants. I was tempted to tell them I'd prove it, but I managed to control my pride. They'll find out in good time.

I climb out of bed a half hour earlier than I had planned. I pause to reflect on my first night sleeping in the kitchen tent, how difficult pulling myself from under the covers had been. I slip out of the kitchen tent and make my way stealthily toward the lab, pausing by the 'Zonlet to fill a canteen, but as I'm bending down at the bank, something makes me pause. Frogs. Maybe a dozen. All floating in the weeds along the bank. I stick my hand in the mud to grab one, and something bites or claws my finger. I pull my hand back and see blood beading up along a half-inch scratch on my index finger. I repeat the process, this time being more careful. I sift through the mud and pull out a piece of glass. I recognize it. It's the vial I buried for Dr. Carter weeks ago. By now, the sap has been completely washed away by the stream. I pick up one of the frogs by the leg and find it stiff. Everything is so alive in the Amazon that death is a puzzling phenomenon. I think back to the toucan, cold and staring. I wish I could stay long enough to run tests.

The lab's screen door squeals as I open it. I hold my breath and listen for the sounds of people stirring, but none come. My eyes adjust to the extreme darkness of the lab. My laptop isn't difficult to find. It's right next to the big desktop computer. I pick it up and I'm set to get the hell out of Dodge, but a thought crosses my mind. I sit down, flip open the laptop, and try to open the SoundZRight program. I get an error message saying, "Cannot Find Application." I run a search. It's completely gone. For a moment I think all is lost, but then I have an idea. Sure, the others may have laughed at my experiments, but Dr. Carter didn't get to where he is by dismissing hypotheses that sound crazy. I flip on the big desktop, cringing as it beeps and clacks its way through the start-up process. Within seconds I've located my research files and the SoundZRight application. He *has* been looking it over. I pull out a blank floppy and copy it back. Then I start to delete the files from the desktop. Before I execute the command though, I decide on a course of action that'll set them back weeks. I scroll down from the special menu and release on "Erase Hard Drive." A dialog box appears.

"Enter Password to Execute."

Damn! I have another idea. I open up my files and start changing my findings. I change "coconut drop" to "leaves rustling." I cut and replace chunks of undefined sounds into the middle of dialog I've already defined. I'd like to do more, but I know I need to get a move on. I reach behind the big computer to shut it off, but as I do, another idea pops into my head. I may not be able to delete any files, but I can copy from one to the other. I find a cable and plug my computer into one of the desktop's ports. I try to copy the entire contents of the hard disk—since I don't know where all the information I need is located—onto mine. I get an error message telling me I don't have enough memory. I calculate the amount of disk space I need. I figure out that there's only one way I'm going to be able to do it. I have to erase everything but my system files from my laptop. *Everything* includes the e-mail program and the modem software.

I don't have much time, but I decide I'd better post one last message home.

> Mom,
> Our Internet server is going down tomorrow.
> Don't worry about me. Everything's great
> here. I may be out of touch for a few
> weeks, but I'll contact you with plane info
> as soon as I can get back online. As soon
> as I get back, I want to hear all about
> your play. Videotape it! Break a leg.
> Grady

I send the message, then get back to business. First, I erase every program and document on my hard drive. That takes several minutes. Then I select all the documents and programs on the mainframe and click on "Copy." A progress bar appears on the middle of the screen. I'm informed that I'm copying 496 files. The desktop provides an estimated loading time of seventy-two minutes. I click on "OK," and the gray bar begins its slow journey across the screen.

Sixty minutes later, I can start to see a glow along the horizon. The sun's not up yet, but it won't be long before someone ventures out of bed. I have a funny thought. Are they expecting me to make breakfast?

But what am I going to spend the rest of the summer doing if not grilling fish and being The Wood Stock Project lackey? Conduct my own research? If I'm going to do that, I need a microphone. I roll my desk chair over to the metal storage closet and twist the handle. It's locked. Since when did they start locking this thing? Probably since Dr. Carter read my research. The keys, I know, are on the ring Dr. Carter carries at all times. The lock on the closet is cheap, just a thin metal bar that slides into place. I know I could pry it open with a crowbar, but there aren't any lying around. I begin scouring the lab for anything I can use to pick the lock, but it's a stupid idea. I can't pick locks. As I'm crossing the lab, I trip over the long orange extension cord that runs from the generators to the power strip in the lab. I know what to do. The progress bar on the computer indicates that I have six minutes left. In the distance, I can hear the buzz of an alarm clock. It shuts off quickly. If all goes according to ritual, that means Jack has just allowed himself his one snooze.

I don't have much time.

I unplug the power strip and wrap the extension cord around the center tent pole several times, then tie off the end. Next, I take the other end of the cord and wind it around the handle of the metal closet. Then I wait. Thirty seconds later, I hear the beep that indicates the computer is finished copying. The next sound is the second buzz of the alarm clock. I'm out of time. I sprint at the tall cabinet and kick it as high as I can, the slack in the extension cord is taken up as the cabinet falls backward. On its way down it runs out of cord, and there's a loud pop as the doors come flying open. The crash of cabinet against floor has probably awakened every living thing in the forest. The pole in the center of the lab has started teetering, and the canvas roof is beginning to cave in. Now I can hear voices. Digging through the contents of the open cabinet, I locate the microphones as well as all the spare laptop batteries. I throw everything into my bag and run.

It isn't quite light outside yet, but the first figure I see as I bolt out the door is recognizable as Roddy. He's wiping sleep from his eyes and yawning. I pass within fifteen feet of him. I think he hears me more than sees me.

"Grady?" he says, surprise registering in his voice.

But I'm by him, and I don't stay to converse.

The next voice I hear belongs to Dr. Carter, and he sounds about one hard-boiled egg away from a coronary. I imagine steam billowing out his ears like on some Popeye cartoon.

"Stop him! STOP HIM!"

Francis emerges from the men's bunk tent, sees me, and takes an angle to cut me off before I hit one of the main trails out of camp, but I've got shoes on, and he doesn't. Plus, I'm already at full speed. I'm five yards ahead of him, and increasing my lead as I head into the thick woods. I'm flying through the forest, barely able to see. Vines and roots and low branches rip at me. I'm climbing higher, toward a clearing that runs along the rim of the basin. The camp can be seen clearly from there. I don't hear Francis behind me, so I slow down long enough to observe what's happening below me. From here, I can see figures moving like plastic soldiers in a sandbox. The canvas roof of the lab has completely collapsed. Dr. Carter fights his way out of it, carrying something in his hand. Inches above my head a tree branch explodes and sends down a shower of wood chips. What follows next is a clap that sounds like thunder. I dive down the trail and roll out of sight of the camp. I pick myself up and sprint.

I can't believe Dr. Carter shot at me.

It's midafternoon by the time I manage to stumble through the heart of the jungle to the Urahwau village. I've been gone less than twenty-four hours. At first I worried that Dr. Carter would assume I would head back here and that he would send a couple of the others after me. I climbed trees twice and waited to see if I was being followed, but no one appeared on the trail. Maybe Dr. Carter just wrote me off as jaguar bait wandering around the forest solo.

Villagers stare blankly at me as I walk through the rows of huts. A couple of the young boys scramble alongside me, laughing and tugging at tattered strips of my shirt, ripped during my flight from camp. Finding Sue is all I can think of though, so I wave them away irritably. I call Sue's name from outside her hut. She gives me a quizzical look when she comes out. "Miss me?" she asks.

I'm so exhausted and flustered, I can't speak at first. She's obviously amused by my stammering and she lets me suffer for a minute before speaking herself. "English. You can do it."

"He shot at me," I say, remembering what I wanted to tell her.

The coy smile disappears from Sue's face. "Who shot at you?"

"Carter," I say.

I proceed to tell Sue all about Dr. Carter wanting to send me home, and about how I got my computer back and ran away. Then about how he tried to shoot me back on the trail.

"Why did he want to send you home?" she asks.

I consider that for a second. Could it really be because I used the microphone and disobeyed orders, or is it something else? Something having to do with my experiments, or with the dead bird and frogs. "Something is wrong about the New Forest. Dr. Carter thinks I know what it is," I say, finally.

"Do you?" asks Sue.

I consider the experiment results all stored safely in the backpack slung over my shoulders.

"Not yet," I say. "Not yet."

For an entire week I work constantly on my sound experiments—adding new commands daily, recognizing the subtleties of the language—and reviewing The Wood Stock Project data, trying to make sense of it. It's slow going, though. Nerve-racking too because I know I'm working against time. If Carter hasn't written me off for dead by now, he must surely be covering his tracks at this very moment, preparing slick responses to any incriminating information I might find.

Just locating the scattered Wood Stock files on the hard drive is only the first step. Many of the ones with more sensitive data are double-encrypted, so I have to go through two separate steps of figuring out the encryption scheme, then laboriously run them through de-encrypt programs. And once I've gone to all this trouble, the files often turn out to be innocuous daily temperature and precipitation reports—stuff that bears no relation to the questions I want answered. Other files are in a database format that can't be read properly with any of the programs on my laptop. I have to open these files in a word-processing program, then pick the numbers out of a sea of random garbage characters. The process is unbelievably tedious, and the operating system crashes often. But the urgency created by my limited battery life—and, I have to admit, my sheer awe at the scope and ambition of Dr. Carter's work—keeps my mind focused.

Much of what I'm seeing indicates that Wood Stock has been an undeniable success in many ways: the oxygen production levels, the growth rates, the health of the trees. After the third day, I began to wonder if I was just being paranoid. The problem is that there's so much data, trying to find what I'm looking for is like trying to find a copy of my dad's doctoral thesis in a reference-less Library of Congress. No one was kind enough to include a helpful file name like, *Incriminating Data*. I'm having to read everything.

I do have my own assistant working with me though—Anru, a boy of about twelve, who has a bright, almost bubbly manner that contrasts with the generally grave demeanor of most Urah-wau males. He looks different too: a bronze cast to his complexion rather than the uniform mahogany brown of the other Indians, and a face that's distinctly oval rather than round. He follows me around as I do my sound experiments, and when I'm waiting around for my three- and four-hour-long de-encryption routines to run on the Wood Stock files. Frankly, even as bright as Anru is, his manic personality, occasionally scatterbrained behavior, and desperate need for approval make him incredibly annoying at times. Like a hyperactive puppy, you don't know whether to pat him on his head or smack him with a rolled-up newspaper. The more I'm around Anru, the easier it is to see why he seems to be so unpopular with the other young people. He's only a year or so younger than me, but I feel much more like his long-suffering big brother than his peer.

I can't begin to guess how much of what I'm doing Anru understands, but he's amazed by both my computer and some of the astounding things I can do with the trees. One of the reasons he likes wandering out into the forest with me is that climbing trees to gather fruit is one of the many duties of young boys. Working with me, the job is reduced to picking the ripe, heavy clusters of fruit and nuts off the ground after I knock them down with my sonic commands. He's begun calling me "Awkye." I ask Sue what it translates to.

"'Keeper of plants,'" she says hesitantly. "No, more than that. One who has a gift with things that grow. What's the expression?" She thinks about it for a moment. "He's calling you . . . well, it doesn't translate exactly to English, but it basically means 'Green Thumb.'"

I'm learning the language of the Urah-wau bit by bit. Anru has taught me about thirty words, mostly functional nouns dealing with food, plants, tools, and weather. Like many of the children, he speaks a little bit of English, and he seems to have a better flair for the language than most. But although we can communicate pretty well in English, I've instructed Anru to make me speak Urah-wau. He's happy with the arrangement. I reward him with a twelve-pack of D-cell batteries that make it possible for him to play songs on a small jambox that was given to him by an American geologist who passed through the village last year. This turns out to be a mistake on my part. The only CD Anru owns is the one he got with the jambox: *ESPN Presents*

GREEN THUMB

Jock Jams, Volume IV. Ever try working out the solution to a complex scientific problem to the accompaniment of Gary Glitter's "Rock and Roll, Part 2"?

Tonight I'm sitting in front of Sue's hut listening to the music being made around the fire. Thanks to this evening's Urah-wau-as-a-Second-Language tutoring session, I now know that the drums are called *timbay*. The small flutes are *lit-zi*. I'm tapping away on the laptop, trying to read as quickly as possible, when the computer beeps to let me know that I'm running out of battery power. It's my fifth of six batteries. I'm nearly out of time. I pause as I try to decide whether to insert the new battery or call it a night. The song they're playing tonight is called "The *Volla-yi*'s Night." The drums are supposed to be the jaguar out on a hunt, but they remind me of a shark, because it has the same sort of beat as the theme from *Jaws*. The *lit-zi* represent the *volla-yi*—the runt of a litter of wild *volla* (tapirs). Anyway, the jaguar is hunting the baby tapir, but through a combination of luck and bravery it manages to avoid getting eaten. The *lit-zi* hit some frantic and wildly paced notes, sort of like "Flight of the Bumblebee" while the *timbay* keep up a relentless and ominous beat. At one point the jaguar has the tapir in his claws, but the *lit-zi* squeal, and the tapir escapes. It's at the exact point when the *lit-zi* hit this high note that I conceive an idea that'll save my battery power and possibly make me the most powerful man in the jungle.

"Anru," I say, getting my protégé's attention. He's wearing one of my T-shirts. It says "Bayside Junior High Honor Society" on it. Anru turns from the fire and looks at me.

"Awkye cle lit-zi," I say.

Green Thumb needs a flute.

Anru has no idea what I'm doing, but he can tell I'm getting frustrated. The idea is simple enough. Use the *lit-zi* to replicate the sound the computer generates. Essentially I need only two notes, so I've reduced the instrument down to two small tubes about three inches long. I can easily hold it in my mouth with no hands and change notes by redirecting my breath with the tip of my tongue. Using a leather strap, I can wear the *lit-zi* around my neck like a traffic cop's whistle. Now I'm slowly hollowing each tube out, making the passageway wider. Anru keeps looking at me with a strange expression, as the *lit-zi* no longer makes any sound that he or I can hear. Still, I keep hollowing out the holes with my pocketknife. I test the *lit-zi* every ten minutes or so, giving the command for trees to bend. So far, I've had no luck.

Anru leans back against a tree and closes his eyes. My work bores him. I continue hollowing out the tube. I'm nervous anyway.

GREEN THUMB

As I scrape another thin layer of porous wood out of the (now pitifully mangled-looking) *lit-zi,* I see Anru lazily open one eye, then the other. I'm about to retest the whistle, but in a blur of movement Anru raises his blowgun, points at my head, and blows. I slam my eyes shut and let out this girlish yelp. A limp seven-foot anaconda falls like a hose down into my lap. A dart is buried between its eyes. Anru points at me and laughs.

"Sampi," I say, using the Urah-wau word for "thank you." I can feel my heart pounding in my chest. I reach down, grab the big snake a few inches below the jaw, and smack its head a couple times against a tree root jutting out of the ground to apply the coup de grâce.

After I manage to settle my rattled nerves a bit, I continue to experiment with the flute. Anru, no longer even remotely bored, is now a rapt spectator. Within a half hour, I'm able to make a branch move in any direction I want. It's time to have fun. I give three short blasts on the high note and one drawn-out low note. One of the vines that's draped over the tree Anru is leaning against begins to move. It winds its way around the tree, binding a squealing Anru to the trunk in the first pass, then continuing to wrap him up. His eyes widen as he giggles, then squeals in mock terror. I blow a silent stop command, and the vine discontinues its mummification of my assistant.

This time, it's my turn to laugh. Anru struggles against the vine. He starts shouting at me in his own tongue. The few words I understand are ones I don't think twelve-year-olds should be using.

As he carries on, a sudden awareness stops my breath and turns my blood to ice. Something's not right. I don't know how I know. I just do. The jungle has its own sounds, smells, even vibrations—the way the wind cuts through the trees. Something is disturbing all of it. I hold a finger up to my lips, hoping the signal is universal. Anru shuts up. There's something, or someone, nearby. A predator. The jungle has the odd, silent calm. The Urah-wau say the jaguar walks in a circle of death, but of course, he never knows it until just before he expires, because he always exists within it. To him, the jungle is a perpetually silent place. I feel like I'm in that circle now. I focus on a jiggling thicket of branches thirty yards from me and blow a noiseless command.

The tangle of branches, vines, roots, and bushes pull themselves away from each other. It's like watching a curtain open. Standing there exposed is an Indian that I would guess is a couple years older than me. I recognize the thick red-and-black stripe that crosses his face. He's Kel-Ha-Nitika, and he's looking at me with awe in his eyes. And why shouldn't he? I am Awkye. I bend the trees to my will.

GREEN THUMB

He appears too petrified to move, and I have no idea what I should do. We stare at each other for a few seconds. I break the silence by belting out Tarzan's battle cry.

The young scout turns and sprints. I have no idea what I'd do if I could catch him, so I let him go. Poor Anru is still pinned to the tree facing the opposite direction. He knows something exciting is going on, but he has no idea what. I blow a command and the vine unwinds, freeing my friend. He stands and swivels his head, scanning the dozens of hiding places surrounding us.

"Unka taysha. Ho unka taysha."

All I know is that *taysha* is the word for "home." Whatever he's saying, it sounds like a good idea to me.

The next night I again sit around the fire listening to the Urah-wau talk, laugh, bang their drums, and play music. As I watch, I silently nurse a cup of *p'yayeh* (semifermented melon juice) and pick at a bowl of stew cooked by the Urah-wau women. The stew is pretty uninspiring. Normally it's made from game the men bring home: monkeys, sloths, various types of unnervingly large rodents. Today, however, it's the same mixture of bland, pasty root vegetables we've had for the previous two days.

Hunting has been pretty slow lately, I learn from Sue. We're in the middle of a drought—a surprisingly common occurrence in the rain forest. The Urah-wau believe this has driven the desirable game animals to higher ground in search of the tender roots and grasses that make up their diet. I wonder, though . . .

"The men will be leaving soon for another hunt," Sue tells me. "This time they could be gone for several days. They intend to follow the *volla* into the hills and see if they have any better luck up there."

Early next morning, preparations for the hunt get underway. Young men are using hammers and big stone chisels to shear long strips of heartwood from a downed tree. From these flat sheets, women and boys with sharp knives are carving arrows, darts, and spear shafts. An old man named Kaawei-Jo, whose specialty seems to be metalwork, is fashioning heads from pounded copper sheets and affixing them to the shafts. Leather packs are being stuffed with pieces of dried meat and fruit, along with a motley assortment of items apparently cadged from Carter's camp: barbecue-flavored Vienna sausages, a jar of Bac*Os, snack-sized packages of peanut butter crackers and—inexplicably—a one-pound log of Velveeta. My stomach involuntarily contracts like a fist.

Elsewhere, other men are spooling a long strand of fibrous green rope around a large stick. Shrieking teenaged boys jab and feint playfully at each other with spears while older, deadly earnest-looking men engage in target practice with bows and blowguns. Women chop brightly colored roots and toss them into a boiling pot, stirring with sticks that glow with almost fluorescent brilliance when lifted from the mix.

Surveying the hunting party, it's pretty obvious that every Urah-wau with XY chromosomes and detectable vital signs is going to be in on the action. Of the roughly twenty males I can see, six look clearly eligible for the Upper Amazon Basin chapter of the AARP. One is suffering from some kind of palsy that causes his limbs to tremble constantly. Two boys who couldn't possibly be any older than eleven solemnly grip blowguns that are a foot taller than they are.

Just for kicks, I join in blowgun practice with the boys who are firing darts into a bull's-eye they've painted on a tree along the riverbank. They're flabbergasted by my marksmanship. Using the long blowguns, after all, is way easier than shooting spit wads.

Sue watches as I outduel the best of the Urah-wau young guns.

"Careful," she says, "or we'll send you out on the hunt."

"Actually, I'd kind of hoped I could go, if you think that'd be possible," I say. "Could you maybe put in a good word for me?"

"So you've hunted before."

"Well, not exactly. Actually, about the closest thing to hunting that I've ever done was help my dad catch a raccoon that was getting into our trash. We sort of cornered him in the garage and held him at bay with Wiffle bats while Mom called Animal Rescue. . . . But still, I can go hours between rest stops and I know all kinds of cool traveling songs and games that'll make the trip less boring. We can sing '99 Bottles of *P'yayeh* on the Wall,' play Red-Sloth/Black-Sloth . . ."

"Grady," Sue said indulgently, "I appreciate that you want to help, but nobody's going to hold it against you if you don't go. You don't owe us anything. You've already thanked us enough for the little bit of help we've given you. Besides, a hunt is a very serious thing. For our men, it's almost a—what's the word for it?—ritual. And are you sure you're really up to paddling a canoe twelve hours at a time, skipping dinner when you're out of food, sleeping on the ground every night . . . ?"

"So you're saying that, if I want to go, nobody's going to try to stop me?"

"What I'm *saying*," Sue says, obviously growing annoyed with me and slowing to emphasize her words, "is that you need to be honest with yourself about whether you really think you can help, or if you're just being a typical man and thinking with, with . . . with something other than your brain."

Man. Hmm. I like that characterization. Especially coming from Sue. But when I reply to her question, I try to sound as matter-of-fact as possible. "Sue, I'm not doing this to show off. And no offense, but I'm not doing it out of gratitude either. I'm doing it because if I try to go up against Dr. Carter alone, it'll be like diving into a tank of piranhas with my pockets full of raw liver. To have any kind of chance at all, I'll need your people's help. But right now, I have no standing whatsoever with these guys. Somehow I've got to make them understand that their old buddy Dr. Carter isn't really the Mister Rogers of the Amazon that they think he is."

I pause for a moment to collect my thoughts before continuing. "There's something else I need to tell you. You know how you said all the animals have headed up into the hills because of the drought? Well, I don't think that's the real reason—or at least it's not the only reason. Think about it: How long have we really been without rain? Only a couple of weeks. I've been in the New Forest recently, and I can tell you there's still plenty of grass and other low-growing vegetation in there. So it's not like there's nothing for the animals to eat. I think that, for some reason, they're *avoiding* eating it. I'm even more sure now than I was before that something's gone wrong with the plant life in Dr. Carter's forest. Seriously wrong. The animals sense that, and they're looking for food elsewhere. . . ."

Sue fixes me with a hard, skeptical gaze, and her mouth opens as if she wants to speak, but she says nothing and I continue.

"So what I have to do is convince your people to help me try to stop Carter from doing—whatever it is he's up to. I know I'm grabbing at straws but I hope that by going along on this hunt, I can build up enough trust so they'll at least listen to what I'm saying."

Sue stares into my eyes for a long, silent moment, then nods almost imperceptibly and walks away. From her noncommittal response, it's hard to tell whether she's impressed by this declaration, but I'm left with the impression that she'll at least vouch for me with the Urah-wau men.

The next day, I learn that Sue has indeed lodged my request to join the hunt. Unfortunately, her endorsement is only the first step. It turns out that this is a call for the Urah-wau council of elders—the leaders of the tribe—to make. My knowledge of Urah-wau civics has by now progressed far enough that I can appreciate what I'm up against.

There are always three members on the council. When one dies, the other two choose the replacement. Currently, the leaders include Klatt-En, Ishoyla, and Monnah. Once a great warrior, Klatt-En's now a half-blind old man. He's still able to catch fish bare-handed from the 'Zonlet, though. Then there's Ishoyla, the old woman who nursed me back to health. She's the closest thing the tribe has to a doctor. She's helped deliver almost every Urah-wau baby in the past half century. The final member of the council is the youngest. His name is Monnah, and it's easy to see by looking at him why he was chosen. He's got the body of a 49ers line-backer and a face that gives away nothing. I've seen him spend entire evenings by the fire without speaking. Normally this might be grounds for thinking someone is dumb, but you can tell by watching Monnah that he's thoughtful. He just doesn't particularly care about the impression he makes on others.

Facing the seated council members in the center of the village, I lay out my case with Sue translating. Basically, I offer a simplified version of what I've already told Sue: The drought is, in my opinion, not the real reason for the bad hunting. There's no shortage of edible plants, especially in the carefully cultivated New Forest, so why aren't the animals eating them? To help uncover the answer, I need to go along on the hunting trip. Perhaps by examining kill from the hunt before they're cleaned and butchered, I can gain some clue as to why these animals have refused to eat plants from Carter's super forest. Or, if some of them have eaten the plants, I can determine what the effects have been.

In my closing argument, I come down hard on the possible long-range results for the Urah-wau. If the *volla* and other game animals migrate away from the village for good, the village will die, or at least be forced to transplant itself wholesale. As for the Urah-wau's relationship with Carter, if he's lied to them about one thing, what else might he be concealing from them? If nothing else, it's essential to dispel any doubt about his true nature and intentions.

What effects my fervent pitch have had on the council members is unclear, because they're totally impassive throughout. And when I'm done, they unceremoniously rise, pick up the mats they've been sitting on, and leave.

"You'll have their decision in the morning," Sue says. "I wish you good luck, Grady, I really do. You haven't necessarily convinced me yet, but you're right about one thing. We need to know the truth, whatever it is."

Later in the day, as the sun begins to ease below the tree line, it occurs to me that I'll probably want to get as much shut-eye as possible tonight, just on the off chance that I'm actually allowed to join the hunt. I stow my leather pouch full of food, water, and traveling supplies in a corner of one of the communal sleeping huts and stretch out on my pallet of woven grasses. Within minutes though, I realize that an early bedtime here will be out of the question. People are still milling loudly outside. Kids are shouting, chasing each other in and out of my less-than-private suite. The normally soothing tones of the *lit-zi* now burrow into my ears like stinging insects. Worse, the heat is unbearable—dry, dusty, and filled with sharp, vinegary aromas emanating from a meat-drying shack adjacent to my hut.

With a grunt of exasperation, I roll up my pallet, push the door flap aside, and disappear into the jungle. I'm soon completely alone, but I'm not afraid. This is a trail I've taken many times. It slowly descends from the hilltop where the Urah-wau village is, winding gently through a narrowing gauntlet of trees and underbrush, and eventually ending on the bank of a broad and shallow stretch of the 'Zonlet.

As I'd hoped, it's dramatically cooler here than in the village. The dust and meaty stench are replaced by the rich protein aromas rising from the coffee-colored stream. The riverbed is strewn with rocks, and as the water flows over them it gurgles and clatters soothingly. I strip to my underwear and wade in. Because the stream is no deeper than six inches here, I don't have to maintain my usual vigilance for snakes or carnivorous fish. The water is a little warm, but it sure feels great splashing over my feet and ankles. I sigh, and the peace of the evening settles over my mind like a soft, weightless blanket. A big, blue waterbird with a shiny green head skims down from the trees and settles on a rock ten feet away from me. Seemingly oblivious to my presence, he snaps sharply at the water with his broad, spatula-like beak. Then, as casually as he arrived, he ruffles his wings and disappears into the coral-colored sunset. The biggest challenge I now face is getting back to the bank before I fall sound asleep on my feet.

My eyes snap open, and the first thing I'm aware of is that it's morning. The second thing is that something alive is on my stomach, creeping slowly upward toward my face. A jolt of adrenaline rips through me like electric current, and I spring to my feet, screaming bloody murder and slapping at my chest and belly. Something clatters to the ground at my feet, and as my vision snaps into focus I see that it's some kind of gray, crabby-looking creature about the size of my hand. Jerking my head from side to side I realize that I'm in the midst of hundreds, maybe thousands, of identical-appearing critters that cover the 'Zonlet's bank and rocky shallows like a living carpet.

My sudden motion has panicked a few of these comical-looking crab things in my immediate vicinity, but the rest go blithely about their morning rounds. They scuffle around in the sandy bank, bask in the sun, lurch over the river rocks that shine like silver in the late dawn light. A few are higher up on the bank, slowly stretching and retracting their jagged little legs like the hippies who do tai chi in the park across from my parents' house. Fascinated, I watch them for a few minutes before deciding I've had enough of this magical Kodak moment. With a loud shriek, I charge into the biggest cluster of the crabs loitering at the water's edge. Galvanized into action, they scramble en masse, kicking up tiny puffs of sand in their flight. Still whooping and flapping my arms, I launch myself into the stream, flushing another big mass of crabs who respond with an equally satisfying display of abject panic.

Then it's back to shore, dashing up and down the bank and watching the crabs sweep away from me in massive waves like flocks of birds flushed from a tree. After maybe three minutes of this retardlike amusement, all the terrorized creatures have retreated into the jungle and I'm standing in the stream, laughing so hard that I'm seriously afraid I'm going to hyperventilate. When I stop breathing though, I still hear laughter. Female laughter. I don't even have to look to know it's Sue.

"Well, Grady," Sue says, wiping tears of mirth from her eyes, "I don't how good a *volla*-hunter you'll be, but you really showed those *to-ach-yai* who's boss! You better hurry back to the village though. The hunting party's about to leave without you."

Yes, it is possible to paddle a canoe upstream. Why anyone in his right mind would want to do so is another question. Anru's nonsensical-sounding answer, "Because it more easy than carry them," hardly puts my curiosity to rest. But after our multigenerational crew of two dozen hunters has traveled about about two miles up the 'Zonlet and entered the awesome main expanse of the Amazon, the answer becomes clear. The jungle along the bank and extending up the hills on either side is so dense that it's impossible to imagine how any ground-bound creature could penetrate it.

The rowing is excruciating, not only in terms of sheer physical strain but also the frustrating amount of distance added by the constant need to zigzag the canoes across the stream in search of slower-moving currents. Fortunately, long-distance rowing seems to have more to do with tenacity and physical endurance than precision motor skills. And, to my pleasant surprise, the muscle packed onto my body by weeks of grunt labor enables me to more or less hold my own with the wiry Urah-wau oarsmen. My fellow huntsmen seem both surprised and mildly impressed, and I luxuriate in a warm, comforting sensation of marginal adequacy.

The first night out, we sleep on a large, dry sandbar about fifty feet from shore. Evidently this is considered preferable to bedding down next to the jungle, because the water provides a natural barrier against midnight visitations by jaguars and the malicious forest demons the Urah-wau believe in with wholehearted conviction. The hunting party's leader, a fellow named Amluk (one of the young guys who was with Sue when she caught me doing my Hans and Franz routine), gives a signal indicating that it's time to eat, and we dig into the sparse stockpile of junk food provisions. Tomorrow, in the interest of preserving our rations, we may have to do without, so I "savor" every stale, crumbly bite of my Lance's toasted cheese crackers, washed down with a few swallows of warm *p'yayeh* from a dented military canteen.

As the campfire gradually spreads through the stack of dry wood and brush scrounged from the nearby woods, I sit down next to Anru. His command of English, limited though it is, is a bond between us. But there's more. It's dawning on me that, even as annoying as Anru is about 90 percent of the time, he's more like me than I care to admit. He's an outsider too. Despite his quick mind, affinity for hard work, and talent with the blowgun, he's pretty much the village pariah, especially among people his own age. Maybe it's his unusual appearance. Or maybe—and this is the explanation that feels most true to me—the other Urah-wau just don't know how to take him. He's interested in all kinds of things that lack obvious practical significance.

One example: Just the other day I watched him spend all day watching a bird build a nest of mud on a large rock overlooking the 'Zonlet. He pointed out to me how the bird would take soft mud from the riverbank and place it at the base of the rock. She wouldn't use the mud right away, he explained. Only after drying for an hour or so in the sun would it be firm enough to use in the nest. He's also become obsessed with my laptop and is particularly taken with the function of the battery: "How put *ekesha* (power) inside?" he asks, turning the mysterious piece of metal and plastic to view it from every angle. "How make stay inside?"

Sitting next to him in the firelight, I see the flames reflected in a silver-colored locket that he wears on a leather cord around his neck. I've noticed it before, but it's never occurred to me to ask what it is. "Show me?" I ask, pointing to the locket.

"Okay Gray-ee," he says, mispronouncing my name in his customary way. He slips the disk over his head and hands it to me. I open it and suddenly understand a lot more about my friend. On one inside surface is a faded color photo of a Hispanic-looking man in the dark fatigues I'd previously seen on American military engineering corpsmen at the Belém airport. He's got his arm around a young, broadly smiling Asian woman who's holding a baby in her arms. The woman's oval face—smooth, bronze-colored, and fringed by short, glossy black hair—is so like Anru's that I gape in fresh awe and wonderment at the miracles contained inside those magical DNA helixes.

"Mutah, fatah," Anru says, underscoring the obvious. "Both lose in big water . . . *flood* when I a baby. Take away in river. I stay with Urah-wau. Anru Urah-wau now." He runs his finger over the photo gently. It's a gesture that seems both tender and halfhearted. Like he realized a long time ago that it has no power to take the sadness away. Before I close the locket, I notice something else. On the opposite side is an inscription. I have to turn the locket toward the fire to read it:

Capt. Andrew Lima, Sr.
Sen-Yi Lima
Andrew Lima, Jr.
4/26/87

Andrew. *Anru.*
"Thank you—*sampi*," I say. "*Sampi,* Anru."

We're up with the chickens (actually macaws

and howler monkeys) in the morning, thanks to Amluk, who rouses us with an outburst of barked exhortations that, I can only assume, translate roughly to, "Rise and shine, maggots!" Still disoriented from deep sleep, we stagger to the canoes and prepare for another twelve hours of aquatic torture. But as it happens, the river gods are with us today. The currents on this stretch of the Amazon are slow and predictable, giving our aching muscles a much-needed rest.

After a couple hours of dead silence broken only by Amluk bellowing commands to his rock-jawed charges, Anru gets bored and hauls out his mud-caked old jambox. He switches it on and skips tracks until he reaches his favorite song, "YMCA." Swiveling his neck with the thumping disco beat, he grins angelically and launches into the classic sports arena routine—which he must have learned from photos on the CD sleeve—of spelling out the title letters with his body. I groan in silent dismay as I take in the contemptuous glares the men are directing at the obliviously boogying Anru.

With a sudden explosion of rage, the warrior sitting behind Anru unleashes a stream of oaths and smacks the jambox with the butt end of his paddle. Batteries scatter across the floor of the canoe, and Anru lurches forward to gather them up.

"Ketche-hayeo! Netateyena pulo!" The guy who kicked the jambox grabs the terrified Anru by the scruff of the neck and shouts into his ear

for at least a minute while the other men smirk and glower. Finally, he shoves the boy away and resumes rowing, muttering under his breath. From the look on his face, I'm sure Anru is about to cry, but in an instant his face changes into something blank, stoic, and unreadable. I know that look pretty well though and I know exactly what it's saying: *I can't be touched now. You can't hurt me anymore.*

Early in the afternoon we reach a stretch of rough water, and Amluk directs us to shore, where we pull up on a narrow bank overhung by a steep stone bluff. This marks the end of our journey's first leg, Anru explains. From here, we'll have to walk the rest of the way to the hunting ground. But first, we have to stow our canoes. Because any rain could raise the water level enough to wash the canoes away from their current position, we'll need to drag them to a big flat ledge near the top of the bluff.

Amluk and another alpha male named Kootah (who seems to be regarded as the Urahwau's resident engineer and handyman) confer briefly, then we get to work. As Anru explains it, most of the men will scale the hill. They'll then throw down ropes, which will be attached to our five canoes and then be used to hoist them up one at a time.

Anru and I draw the job of staying below and tying the ropes to the canoes, one each on the fore and aft ends. The work goes fast, and as Anru finishes loading the final canoe with the food and provisions, I begin my climb up the hill. I'm within ten feet of the top when a chorus of agitated cries erupts from directly above. *"Yetata! Yetata!"* This is followed by a dull, creaking noise, then a shower of cans, boxes, and plastic-wrapped packages crashing down on my head and shoulders. It's our food bundle tumbling out of the last canoe. Grabbing wildly with my free hand, I manage to snag the Velveeta box, but everything else rattles oversurging white water of the river. One of the knots—the one Anru tied to the back of the canoe—has obviously come loose, allowing the free end to drop and tip the food sack out.

Tucking the cheese box under my armpit, I finish scrambling to the top, where the men are hauling the now-empty canoe over the brink of the cliff.

"Doyese-Ita! Suri ay nese de doyeye?" shouts the clearly livid Amluk, pointing to the dangling ends of the untied knot.

"What's he saying?" I ask Anru, who's just now reaching the summit.

Anru tries to say something but manages only a high, crooning noise from deep in his throat.

"Hey, come on, Anru! You've gotta tell me what he's saying!"

"Amluk want to know . . . ," Anru says in a

trembling voice. "He want to know who make knot to hold boat."

From the expressions the men are directing at Anru, it's pretty clear that everyone already knows the answer to that question.

The one bright spot in this situation is that our schedule is apparently too tight to squeeze in a daylong mass beat-down of poor Anru. Our food is virtually gone, so the immediate order of business is to rustle up something, *anything,* to sustain us for the rest of the hunt. We need to get this done quickly, Amluk says, so we can cover a few more miles before dark. Anru and I, now even more emphatically ostracized by the rest of the party, forage together.

After an indefinite period of aimless wandering in the jungle, Anru suddenly snaps to life and starts hopping excitedly, pointing into the high branches of a tree directly ahead of us. "Gray-ee, look! *Monache!*"

It takes me a few seconds to figure out what he's pointing at, but then I see. The tree is chock-full of *monache*—big, clustering fruits that look something like oversized guava but taste like the richest, sweetest peaches you've ever had. They're one of the few types of jungle-growing fruit that I'm actively enthusiastic about. The only problem is that the *monache* tree is both tall and covered with sharp spines that make climbing almost impossible. And since the trunk is too thick to shake, the only way to harvest the fruit is to wait until they're blown down by wind.

But then I'm struck by the obvious: I'm not just some hapless *Kaawei-Jo* six-pack. I'm *Awkye*. Green Thumb. Lord of all leafy lieges. Undisputed mack daddy of the Upper Amazon Basin 'hood. I pull my *lit-zi* from my backpack, wet my lips, and play a couple of warm-up notes. Then I start directing short, staccato blasts at the tree's upper branches. Possibly because the fruit-bearing branches are so high, I don't immediately get the response I want, but before long the limbs are swaying as if a wayward Texas tornado has lit into them. Soon, one of the biggest *monache* clusters has started working its way loose and, with an emphatic snapping sound, it separates from its branch. Anru, who's already bug-eyed from excitement, positions himself under the plunging clump of fruit like a Dodger outfielder tracking a lazy fly ball.

As the *monache* hurtles groundward, I suddenly groan with a clear recognition of what's about to happen. This *monache* cluster isn't just big; it's huge, easily the width and breadth of a dorm-room refrigerator. Anru, having had the same realization, gulps visibly. He looks for all the world like Wile E. Coyote looking up haplessly as the shadow of a falling boulder expands around him. But he stands his ground.

When the clump of bowling ball–sized fruit

crashes into Anru with a thunderous *wump!* it drives him to the turf like a Doc Martens boot on a cockroach. I immediately scramble over and plunge my hand into the pulpy pile of shattered *monache*. I feel around until I locate Anru's arm and use it to pull him to a sitting position.

"Hey, Anru, are you all right?" I ask.

Anru gives his head a couple vigorous shakes, slinging chunks of bright yellow pulp everywhere, then he spits a flap of *monache* peel from his mouth and gives me a bright, toothy grin. "I make nice catch, huh Gray-ee?" he says.

"Yeah, real nice grab, buddy," I say, helping Anru to his feet while silently thanking the fates for blessing my sunny-tempered friend with a short attention span.

When we rendezvous with the other hunters, our double armloads of *monache* (about ten of the fruit survived the drop unbroken) draw grudging nods of approval. Their haul is pretty meager: a couple of water rats, several large frogs, some wild root vegetables, and a burlap bag full of something that feels warm and spongy to the touch. We stash the canoes in the underbrush and start walking. The terrain goes steadily uphill from this point, but at least the riverbank is wide enough to walk on now, so we don't have to hack our way through the jungle.

"We close now," says Anru. "*Volla* come here when no rain. We kill two, maybe three, then go home."

ROB THOMAS

Night is closing in, but something weird is happening. The horizon directly ahead is growing brighter rather than darker. The reason becomes clear when the wind changes direction and a massive blanket of inky-black smoke rolls over the tree line. We top a hill, and I gasp in disbelief at what I see. Stretched for about a mile along the riverside and as deep into the receding valley as I can see, the rain forest is on fire. Helicopters, their bright searchlight beams dancing and crossing in the night sky, circle over the roaring orange expanses. Occasionally, one will eject a silvery stream of water that explodes into a dense steam cloud on contact with the fire, but has no other apparent effect. As we walk along the shoreline, now within one hundred yards of the blaze, bright cinders swirl to earth all around us. They hiss and snap as they settle into the river. Shouts—in Portuguese, English, and some language I can't understand—rise from the periphery of the blaze. Radio static crackles from a truck that bears an insignia of the Brazilian flag.

What strikes me as we walk along the shore, our outlines silhouetted against the fiery backdrop and our shadows stretching long on the flat, sandy bank, is how nonchalant my companions seem about all this. It's nothing they haven't seen before, I guess. We walk on for perhaps another mile or two, just enough so that the flames from the wildfire are reduced to a pulsing glow in the southern sky. Then Amluk shouts the command to make camp. As I work, I keep stealing glances at the unnatural aurora borealis that lights up the jungle night. I imagine myself in a low-orbit photomapping satellite, creeping around the earth's endless horizon, seeing scores of dense orange-and-black clusters spreading slowly inside shrinking fields of emerald. I've always winced whenever my dad's friends slap me on the back and say, "Botany, huh? Well, son, it looks like you're getting into a real *growth field.*" I considered their little joke factually accurate, if somewhat lame. Now I'm not so sure of the accuracy. Maybe a deal with the devil is our only hope. And maybe the devil we need is the very one who brought me to this place.

After the mentally and physically harrowing day we've had, I'm hungry enough to eat dirt. But even so, I've got to say that the brace of bucktoothed water rats Kootah's roasting on a spit don't look all *that* much more appetizing than a big bowl full of sandy loam. More intriguing to me is the fare that a rival chef, Nitizi, is whipping up. Close examination reveals that it's a kind of shish kebab of frog legs and—excellent!—some of the very same land crab critters, the *to-ach-yai,* that I was harassing the other morning. These, obviously, were the mysterious contents of the burlap bag. Nitizi's Surf 'n' Turf

Special tastes even better than it looks. The frog legs are pretty decent, but the *to-ach-yai* are to die for. They're even better than the $14.95 Alaskan king crab plate that Dad lets me order at Red Lobster when I turn in an all-A report card. Next to the rack of kebabs is a pan filled with melted Velveeta. The assembled chow hounds are using it as a dipping sauce for their charbroiled meat. Mom—she of the tofu salads, unsweetened mueslix breakfast cereals, and "heart-smart" frozen pasta entrées—would blow out a cerebral artery if she could see me eating this gloppy, cinder-encrusted feast.

"People back home would go nuts over this stuff if they could get a taste of it," I tell Anru, chunks of crab leg and Velveeta escaping from my mouth as I speak. "Do you know if these crabs live in other places or just in the jungle around here?"

"Crab?" Anru repeats, puzzled at first by the word. Then a grin of recognition creeps across his face. "Crab! Like this, eh?" He pantomimes crablike pincer movements with his hands. "No no no. This not crab. This spider! Maybe a little like—how I say it?—tarantula!"

Now I have two choices. I can follow my first instinct, bolt into the jungle, and heave my guts out until every last loathsome molecule of insectoid matter is flushed from my stomach—thus losing face for the second time in a day and probably becoming a standard foil for all future generations of Urah-wau stand-up comics. Or . . .

With every ounce of self-control I can muster I slowly ease another *to-ach-yai* off my kebab stick. I hold it up in the light and examine its glistening spread of eight fat, juicy legs, wondering why I hadn't noticed the hairiness of their upper legs before. Then I rub it around the bottom of the Velveeta pan, sopping up the last few drops of golden cheeselike goodness. I wait until I know I can speak with some semblance of a casual, offhanded tone. "Spider, huh? Could've fooled me."

It's show time!

Volla Fest '99 is now fully underway, and the general sense of dull exhaustion we've all labored under for the past couple days is lost in the primal male frenzy of preparing to go forth and kill things. The Urah-wau are seriously pumped at the prospect of unchecked carnage and mayhem. And, as ashamed as I am to admit it, so am I.

Amluk has divided us into separate parties. All, I note, are admirable mixes of youth, age, and various levels of physical capacity. Though at times he can be an overbearing jerk, I have to admit that Amluk has a real knack for rational leadership. But, I'm a bit peeved to notice Anru and I have been assigned to the only group that has seven members instead of six. What's more, the other five members are all healthy guys in their physical prime, and all have excellent marksmanship skills. Apparently, Anru and I are our group's designated spazzes. Thanks for the vote of confidence, Amluk!

No more than forty-five minutes have passed in the forest before Keke, a big strapping teenager, nails a small *volla* with a jaw-dropping forty-yard heave of his spear. General exultation erupts, and Keke—who's obviously walking on air at his accomplishment—gets to cut off the animal's tail as a souvenir of his first kill.

Things calm down in a hurry though, as the small herds of *volla*, evidently alerted to the threat we pose, now bolt whenever we get anywhere near them. We do, however, find a couple of decaying carcasses of *volla* who don't seem to have suffered any physical injuries. I think back to the dead toucan in the New Forest, and more fuel is added to my suspicion the animals of the Basin have knowledge about Carter's great experiment that has so far eluded my grasp.

Nitizi, the leader of our group, is in the process of suggesting that we split up to make ourselves less conspicuous, when a loud snapping noise from the hill above us causes us all to turn in unison. An enormous *volla,* easily the biggest we've seen all day, is scrambling up the rock-strewn slope. He's well out of range now, even for Elway-armed Keke. However, the way he's skidding and slipping in his panicked flight makes it clear that we have a realistic chance to close the distance fast.

GREEN THUMB

Anru and I are nearest to the hill, so we get a head start. Popping a dart into my blowgun as I clamber up the hillside, I find a stretch of pebble-free ground and, in an instant, I'm within twenty yards of the laboring beast. But before I can find a spot to set up for a blowgun shot, the *volla* disappears into a line of trees about halfway up the rise. As we continue upward, I notice that none of the others have been as nifty as we have in avoiding the crumbly field of gravel. The blood pounds in my head and chest as I realize: It's all up to me now.

As we approach the tree line, I can see that it's a hopelessly impenetrable mass of vegetation. But in a decision that seems to flash from a scary-fast, computer-enhanced RoboGrady brain, I instantly know what to do. The *lit-zi* flies to my mouth, and when we reach the trees we don't even have to slow down. The limbs and creepers have already parted before us, creating a passageway that clears our bodies by maybe two feet on all sides. Anru whoops with delight. The sound of the branches sweeping apart in front of us is like waves rushing up on the beach. It's spooky and thrilling at the same time. So is the darkness in our moist, steamy tunnel— only a few tiny patches of sunlight penetrate the emerald dreamscape I'm moving through.

I know we're close on the *volla*'s heels. Every now and then the vegetation flows apart to reveal him galloping along, his flanks shiny with sweat and his head lowered like a battering ram. As thrilling as this is, I know I can't keep it up much longer. The *volla,* recognizing his place in the food chain, is far more motivated than I am. Furthermore, he doesn't have to waste his precious wind by blasting incessantly on a flute as he runs. Just as this thought passes through my mind, we burst into the open air, and I nearly stumble and fall in the blinding sunlight. Straight ahead is an even steeper rise than the one we've been climbing. The *volla,* seeming to shift into a new gear, lets out a sudden, guttural honk and attacks the slope with a vengeance. We're still right on his tail though. And because I no longer have to riff along on my *lit-zi* as I run, I feel like I'm getting a second wind.

Okay, here's the moment of truth. We're close to the top of the hill. More importantly, we've entered a narrow ravine that funnels us straight upward toward a flat-floored cul-de-sac blocked off in back by a large fallen tree. End of the line.

Warily, Anru and I creep up to within twenty feet of the *volla*—now slumped in seeming exhaustion at the base of the fallen tree.

I motion to Anru to stay where he is, then I slowly move a few feet closer. Trying to avoid sudden motion, I reach for my blowgun and raise it to my mouth. The *volla* appears to be regarding me with calm resignation, his stubby, trunklike nose quivering as he draws breaths in with loud, spasmodic snuffles. For some reason I become aware that he has these amazingly clear, intelligent-looking eyes, and that they're topped by a fringe of delicate black lashes. This is definitely not what I need to be dwelling on now. Reaching inside for something ancient and pitiless in my nature, I try to force myself to regard him only as prey. I inhale a deep ragged lungful of air, then let it explode through the blowgun.

Nothing.

At first I think I've missed. But how? It's a total point-blank shot that I could make with my eyes closed. Even the *volla* seems taken aback, blinking at me as if to ask, *Hey, what happened?*

Then I realize. The dart has fallen out of the tube during the chase. I reach into my pouch for a new dart, but the *volla* has no intention of waiting quietly while I load up for another shot. He lurches to his feet, puts his head down like a fighting bull, and charges straight for me.

I don't have time to wimp out. The only thought on my mind is the absolute need to block the *volla*'s escape route. When he crashes into my gut it feels like Ed Stimmons's pile-driver fist taken to the tenth power. I tumble backward, dazed by the impact. But as the *volla* is galloping over my prostrate body I somehow have the presence of mind to reach up and grab hold of one of his skinny shanks. With a hard yank, I not only manage to flip myself back onto my stomach but trip the startled *volla*. Before he can recover, I throw myself on top of him like a sumo wrestler, wrapping one arm around his neck in a not-too-effective choke hold attempt while gripping one of his front legs with the other. It's pretty much a blur from this point on. All I'm aware of is spinning, heaving, flailing, and Anru's falsetto squeals in the background. Sudden, jarring impacts with the ravine's rock wall are followed by a forward roll into a hot, fetid mud hole. There's nothing I want to do more than let go and make this ridiculous carnival ride stop, but short of death, nothing's going to make me do that.

With a sudden, blinding forward rush interrupted by the brain-jarring impact of caked dirt against my face, Round One comes to an end. Somehow, I've ended up right back where I started, guarding the downhill exit route while the *volla* regards me from the base of the deadfall. He's finally managed to throw me off, but he hasn't got enough strength left to make his escape. About ten feet away, I can see Anru lying in a heap on the ground, apparently knocked senseless during the *volla*'s rampage. I quickly ascertain that my friend is breathing more or less normally, and that all of his major limbs are still attached. Thus reassured, I turn my attention back to the *volla*. Gasping in perfect unison, the sweat-flecked beast and I gaze at each other with equivalent *now*-what-*exactly-was-the-point-of-this-exercise?* looks.

GREEN THUMB

Novice though I am at this, I've already gained one crucial insight into *volla* hunting: He who tries to wrestle 350-pound jungle swine into submission had best develop a taste for vegetarian cuisine. Time to play it smart. Taking care to avoid sudden movement, I grab my *lit-zi,* dust it off, and play a command that unfurls a fat creeper from a tree overhanging the ravine. My impromptu strategy is to try to loop the vine around the *volla's* legs or hindquarters, but I realize the vine is shorter than it looked from the ground. The effort of stretching the vine toward the *volla* is causing the tree branches to rustle, so I try to distract the animal by gazing intently into his eyes and babbling soothing nonsense— vaguely conscious as I do so of how ridiculous this situation would look to someone who just happened onto the scene.

"Gooood pig, nice pig, *keep looking at me* . . . that's good. Just relax that lower lip and keep that vacant stare going . . . yeah, that's a gooood boy. I can just hear those *volla* brain waves flatlining out right now: *zeeeeee* . . ."

Suddenly, the animal stirs, and I realize I'll lose him if I don't act immediately. I blast a command for the creeper to extend and coil, and it just manages to loop around the upper portion of one of the *volla's* hind legs an instant before he gets away. The creature bellows with rage and starts charging around in a semicircle, straining violently against the taut vine. While he's occupied, I hurriedly pry a big rock loose from the bottom of the mud hole and try to get close enough to conk the *volla* on the head.

I can't reach him though, because he's started trying to scramble up a ladder of broken branches and escape over the deadfall. Groaning at the prospect of losing my prey, I stagger up after him. As I climb, I feel the sharp pain of broken sticks piercing my flesh. When I'm right up next to the furiously thrashing creature, I raise the stone over my head with trembling arms and scream in preparation for bringing it down on his skull. However, at that precise moment, the creeper snaps and the *volla* is free. His forward momentum suddenly unfettered, he rockets upward with startling speed, reaching the top of the deadfall in a couple bounds. Digging his hooves into the tree trunk, he vaults toward the other side and disappears from view.

There's a moment of perfect silence. Then a piercing, echoing squeal rises from behind the deadfall, seeming to recede in the distance with impossible speed. Exhausted, but even more mystified, I clamber over the mass of shattered branches. I'm about to hop down, when I realize that would be a very serious mistake. Instead of solid ground beneath my feet there's about seventy feet of sheer, vertical cliff looming above the main fork of the Amazon River. At the base of the cliff, on an otherwise empty mound of sand, is the sprawling carcass of a *volla* who—I sincerely hope—died of fright long before he hit the ground.

I guess I should be feeling pretty good about this. Anru certainly is. But then, he's the one whooping like a maniac while crowd-surfing on the hands of his jubilant fellow hunters, and I'm the one sitting on a tree stump watching the whole thing in solitary silence. While the festivities rage, I glumly busy myself bagging and sealing tissue samples from the *volla,* along with food particles I've taken from his stomach. I'll check them out when I get back to the village, but without a microscope it's going to be tough to draw any definitive conclusions about what it is about the New Forest vegetation that makes the animals go to such great lengths to avoid it.

Altruism, I decide, is overrated. Guess I should've figured that out before I gave Anru the credit for wrestling the *volla* over the cliff's edge. In fairness to Anru, he clearly doubted the yarn I had him tell Amluk and the others—although, since he'd only recently emerged from a daze at the time, who was he to say any different? As far as he knew, he really might've been the one waging the death-struggle with the runaway beast while I cheered him on from the sideline. My main source of annoyance, I realize, is how quick the Urah-wau were to accept even the geekish Anru as a more likely candidate for heroism than me. I sure hope D. V. is right about that karma stuff, that this big moment for Anru was worth blowing an easy shot at ingratiating myself with the Urah-wau men.

Still, looking at Anru's ecstatic face, I can't feel too bad about what I've done. Having been credited with killing what may well be the all-time Urah-wau Game Commission–certified trophy *volla* boar, the little guy is getting the total "we're not wortheee!" treatment. This from the very same knuckleheads who were shunning him only hours earlier. But, of course, we leper-nerd types are a pretty tight brotherhood, so in a sense a triumph for one of us is a triumph for all. The guys are all so awed by his accomplishment that they don't even make him help drag the sled bearing the massive *volla* carcass back to the place where we stashed the canoes.

Apart from my uncredited kill and Keke's, we've managed to bag only one more runty *volla* before leaving. However, from what Anru says, our big fella has already made this hunt a success of historic magnitude. And all false modesty aside, I've got to say that this is in fact one enormous pig. So big, he has to be strapped across two lashed-together canoes to be transported downstream.

Since the river's current is now working with us, we hardly have to paddle at all, and our trip home becomes a nonstop floating party. The *p'yayeh* flows freely, and the insistent *thumpa-thumpa thumpa-thump* beat of "Rock and Roll,

Part 2" from Anru's (now fully sanctioned) jam-box echoes through the river valley, punctuated by our lusty unison *Hey!*s. It occurs to me that I'll never feel any need to pledge a frat in college. I've already had the whole experience concentrated into one four-day outing at age thirteen.

Very likely it's just my stubborn refusal to admit anything I've ever done was wrong, but I'm starting to feel pretty good about myself now. Maybe better than I've ever felt before. It doesn't make sense when you look at it rationally. Four days have passed on this hunt, and I'm still not one bit closer to gaining the credibility I'll need to turn the Urah-wau against Carter. My first reflex as a scientist is to try to analyze myself, figure out why I'm having this illogical emotional response. It could be that simply admitting I would've liked a little appreciation for what I've done—a little of the respect I've clearly earned—has been a liberating experience in itself. It's proof that I'm not as different from everyone else as I've always fancied myself. Though I haven't got it all worked out in my mind yet, something tells me this is a positive development.

Then, something else tells me to stop all this thinking and just enjoy the moment.

And I do.

The first night after our return, Sue leaves me to celebrate with the rest of the men. First thing in the morning though, she's in my tent with five days' worth of accumulated questions. I'm seated cross-legged on the floor, treating tissue samples from the *volla* with reagents I've extracted from indigenous root vegetables. I've gotten some interesting reactions that indicate chemical peculiarities in the animal's blood, and the stomach lining was covered with odd, clearly unusual white spots and lesions. Unfortunately, due to the primitive nature of my equipment and methods, it's probably nothing that would stand up in court.

Sue's questions don't deal with my tests though. Her curiosity deals with a longer-range issue I've overlooked in my obsession with the New Forest's biology. What recommendations, Sue is asking, will Dr. Carter give regarding development of the rain forest?

As I think about it, it dawns on me how this will play out. The more successful the New Forest is, the more acres of the current forest can be destroyed. It's such an American way of measuring success. The oxygen we need will be produced. The cattle we eat can graze on the bulldozed forest. Who cares about what will happen to the people who live on the land?

"Have you seen the New Forest?" I ask?

"From a distance," Sue responds. "Dr. Carter has warned us that we could damage the experiments if we venture inside."

But what could they possibly hurt? I wonder—not for the first time—if the full truth of what's going on around here isn't stashed away deep within Dr. Carter's gated and barred mind.

It's late the following afternoon when I finally find the mother lode: the specific documents I've been looking for since I made off with the Wood Stock files. Dr. Carter has hidden them in a folder innocuously titled "Supply Budget." All the details I'm looking for exist within. Inside I learn that despite the tremendous growth and remarkable health of the trees, the complete ecosystem has failed to return. The dissemination of seeds, normally handled by mammals and birds, has not taken place at all. Dr. Carter and Sonja have hand-planted every super tree in the forest. In other words, the jungle wouldn't be self-perpetuating. It would require a team of scientists to maintain. That, in itself, might doom The Wood Stock Project, but there's more. The reason that wildlife hasn't moved into the

New Forest is that the chemicals pumped into the super trees to achieve the amazing growth are toxic. They immediately attack white blood cells. Naturally, Dr. Carter has taken thorough notes, even about his own failure. If only I could get this to someone back in America.

> UNCONTROLLED GROWTH OF THE INSECT POPULATION—MOST SPECIES OF WHICH ARE IMMUNE TO THE TOXINS' EFFECTS—RESULTS DIRECTLY FROM A NEAR-TOTAL ABSENCE OF PREDATORS WITHIN THE NEW FOREST. THE BATS, ANTEATERS, MONKEYS, ETC., THAT LIVE ON THESE INSECTS TYPICALLY DIE WITHIN TWO HOURS AFTER INGESTION OF SPECIES THAT SUBSIST ON LEAVES, FRUIT, BARK, AND SAP. DIRECT CONSUMPTION OF LEAVES, FRUIT, ETC., INVARIABLY RESULTS IN DEATH WITHIN FIVE TO TEN MINUTES. EVEN THE INGESTION OF GRASSES AND OTHER VEGETATION THAT CONTAIN TRACE AMOUNTS OF THE ENHANCEMENT FORMULA CAN RESULT IN MORTALITY TO LARGER SPECIES SUCH AS SLOTHS AND TAPIRS WITHIN FORTY-EIGHT TO SEVENTY-TWO HOURS.

The computer beeps, warning me my battery power is low. I run out to get Sue. She's not in her hut. I scramble around the village until I find her stirring this giant cauldron hanging above a fire. Something smells atrocious. I ignore whatever it is she's doing and I hold up the screen in front of her. "Read," I say.

She hands the stir stick off to one of the other girls and sits down on a nearby log. I watch her as she scrolls through the documents. "I'll tell the council," she says somewhat absently. Then she turns her sad eyes up to me. "Grady, how do we stop them from doing this?"

"I don't know," I say honestly. "They're going to bring in all the members of the commission so they can show off the New Forest. We've got to prove that it's a lie."

"How can we do that?"

I shrug.

"When are they coming?"

"I don't know."

There's a long pause while the two of us sit there contemplating what a positive report by the commission will mean to the rain forest. Finally, Sue speaks. "Is it possible that Dr. Carter would have notes in these files about when the group is coming?"

I think about it. "Yeah," I say, allowing myself to get a little excited. "His e-mail files are on here. That's the way he keeps in touch with all the members of the commission. Hand me that."

I take the laptop back from Sue and begin

clicking away. I open up the incoming e-mail folder. I recognize some of the e-mail addresses as belonging to commission members. I scroll down until I get to the most recent files, then I begin scanning the subject headings. Finally I see one that says, "Plane reservations."

"It's here," I say to Sue.

I double-click, but as I do the screen on my laptop goes black. My last battery is dead.

Sue and I just stare at the computer for several minutes like we can telepathically recharge the battery. Finally she gets up dejectedly. She campaigned so hard for the Urah-wau to help The Wood Stock Project that I know she's reluctant to go admit what's happened. She's told me there are those in the tribe who resent how much influence she has with the tribal council.

Evidently, Sue's pessimism is well-founded. After more than an hour of deliberation, the council decides to continue cooperating as usual with The Wood Stock Project until I can demonstrate to their satisfaction that Dr. Carter isn't looking out for their best interests. My participation in the hunt, after all, has so far failed to yield anything they'd accept as proof of his bad intentions. And as I've quickly discovered, the facts and implications in the computer files are hopelessly incomprehensible to them.

When the Urah-wau last delivered supplies to the project, Dr. Carter asked whether I was staying with them. Sue told him no, of course, but she said she could tell that Dr. Carter didn't believe her. He told her that I had stolen wallets, watches, and computer equipment from the scientists, and they'd learned that I had a criminal record back in the United States. He said that was why he was trying to send me home. In front of me, Sue acted like she didn't believe him, but what proof have I offered that what he said wasn't true? She could see the six batteries I had. She might assume I've simply hidden the watches and wallets somewhere in the jungle.

"The council doesn't believe what you're saying about Dr. Carter," Sue says resignedly. "They say that Dr. Carter has always been helpful to us. He's given us supplies, medicine. They pointed out that you did have the batteries Dr. Carter says you stole."

"You saw it though!" I say. "You saw Dr. Carter's notes. You know I'm not lying."

"Grady, all I saw were words. I didn't see who wrote them."

"So you don't believe me either?"

"I didn't say that," she says. "I do believe you. The others of my tribe don't speak English; they only hear the sound of Dr. Carter's voice. I can tell in the words he chooses and the way he speaks them that he cares more for his own well-being than that of others living far from what he would call civilization."

"So what do we do?" I ask. "How do we convince the rest of the tribe that Dr. Carter isn't their ally?"

"We need to do two things," Sue says. "We need to take the members of the council into the New Forest. I think I can convince them to do that. Plus, we need to find out when the people from the commission will be visiting."

"I need another battery to find that."

"Grady," Sue says, "there's no way you're going to get back into that camp again."

The council has agreed to venture into the New Forest and decide for themselves whether Dr. Carter is an ally or an enemy. With both Klatt-En and Ishoyla making the three-mile trek to the New Forest, the travel is slow. A small party of the strongest men, known as *bwayna* (a multipurpose Urah-wau word meaning both "hunter" and "warrior"), accompany the council. Anru begged to go, but Monnah shook his head no. After that, Anru said no more. As we set out, I told Sue to tell the others not to eat anything in the New Forest. She makes the announcement. The others exchange curious glances, but nod agreement.

All the *bwayna* are armed with both blow-guns and bows. I'm carrying a blowgun. I've taken to traveling shoeless like the Urah-wau, and though it was painful at first, the bottoms of my feet have built up thick calluses, and now I'm able to move nearly as silently as Anru, though I'm not even in the same league as Sue.

We make it to the edge of the jungle by late

afternoon where Amluk, who's been scouting the area, joins us. There we hide in the trees and wait. Again I'm awed by both the devastation of the clear-cutting that turned thousands of acres into a dust bowl, and by the incredible oasis Dr. Carter has genetically engineered in the middle of it all. I have to remind myself that it's a sham. I remember hearing a story once about an adviser to a Russian czarina who constructed cheerful facades for dilapidated buildings and ordered the peasants, under threat of death, to smile and cheer as the czarina passed through their towns. The ruse was devised to convince her that his reforms were working and the people were happy. That's what this forest is. It might look stunning, but it's a facade.

No one speaks for nearly an hour. Finally I hear the air-horn blast that summons all the members of The Wood Stock Project to the edge of the New Forest. We're patient as they assemble five or six hundred yards away from us, then head directly away from us toward their own camp. No one moves until Monnah gives a command some fifteen or twenty minutes later. I swing down from the branch I've been squatting on, reach down to a lower branch, then let myself drop lightly to the ground.

Our party ventures out across the wasteland. I notice the others staring up at the spectacular trees, wondering to themselves what could be wrong with anything so majestic. The Urah-wau

use the same word for "magic" and "science"—
yulo. I understand why, to them, the difference
between science and magic is only a semantic
one. Even if you could sit down and go over
every theory, every chemical that goes into the
process, and even if the Urah-wau *bwayna* you
explained it to grasped every concept, it would
still be *yulo*.

We enter the New Forest, and the party splits
up. They begin touching the flora like they're
walking through some sort of museum. It's one
thing for me to stumble onto this spot, but I try
to put myself in their position. Three years ago,
there was nothing here. Now this. I keep my
eyes focused on the ground. I'm looking for evi-
dence. I'm looking for death: bats, birds, monkeys. Sue is walking nearby.

"It's quiet," she says.

"Yeah . . . too quiet," I retort, but then I
realize she won't get the joke. She hasn't
watched as much bad television as I have. In
fact, she hasn't watched any. She takes my comment at face value.

"You're right," she says. "There are no animals. We should be able to hear them, even if we
can't see them."

"What the tribe needs to understand is that
at the speed these trees are growing, the freak-
ish sizes they're reaching—they hurt the Urah-
wau. It gives the government the excuse it wants
to wipe out more of the rain forest. They'll jus-

tify it to the world community by planting more of Dr. Carter's biologically enhanced trees."

We've made it to what I'd estimate to be the center of the New Forest. Interestingly, it's perhaps even a little darker here than in the rest of the jungle. The thickness of the branches, the preponderance of leaves on the super trees; somehow, the New Forest is spookier. I glance around at the dozen Urah-wau performing their own version of a scientific study. The medicine woman, Ishoyla, pulling one of the smaller vines up by the root and sniffing it. A couple of the *bwayna* using a machete to strip away the bark of one of the largest trees. I turn my attention to Amluk, who's largely shielded from my view. He's standing underneath a fruit tree that produces these smallish bananas. Looking around, there are a dozen fruit trees in a fifty-foot radius, trees that don't belong in the Amazon, trees that don't even belong in the Southern Hemisphere. The lowest banana tree branches hang down to about eight feet off the ground. He's holding one of the fruit in his hand. It takes a second for me to realize what's happening.

"DON'T!" I shout.

But the word means nothing to Amluk, who stuffs half the fruit into his mouth. He looks over at me and smiles. I think he thinks I'm playing some sort of game. Maybe he thinks I want one too. He jumps up in order to grab another fruit off the tree, but he misses on the first try. I whistle on my *lit-zi* as he coils to jump again. The tree's branches bend up with all the flexibility possible. The bananas are safely out of his reach.

The other Urah-wau turn their gaze to me. They have no idea what just happened to the tree, but they get the idea that I somehow caused it.

"Grady?" Sue says to me.

"Stick a finger down Amluk's throat," I shout.

Sue barks out something in her native language, but I realize that's only going to be a momentary reprieve from answering the question that's on everybody's mind. I don't have to answer anything right away, however, because the next thing we hear are drums. They're all around us, and they're beating out a rhythm of war. I've never heard anything like it, but I know it's meant to frighten us. I can't speak for the others, but it's working on me. All the Urah-wau freeze, but only momentarily. The *bwayna* surround the two older council members. I get the impression they'd also like to shield Monnah, but he's having nothing to do with that. He's already pulled his machete out.

Then I see them. They ease out of the darkest corners of the jungle. The circular band of red-and-black paint around their heads identifying them as Kel-Ha-Nitika. The first words of an order come from Monnah's mouth, but they're cut off by his scream when an arrow imbeds itself into his shoulder. I'm standing behind him at the time, and I can see the bloody tip sticking out his back. He collapses to the ground and writhes in agony. The Kel-Ha-Nitika step closer. There must be a dozen of them moving stealthily toward us. They stop when they're within ten yards. One order from their leader and we could all be cut down before we blinked. But the Indian who speaks is the last one we'd expect. Strangely enough, I think I know him. It's the young, thin one that Anru and I caught spying on us. He speaks in the language of the Urah-wau. I recognize two or three of the words, and I realize I am the subject of the command.

When the teenager finishes with the terms, Sue shouts back at him.

"Rah!"

It's the Urah-wau word for "no."

But blind Klatt-En shushes Sue harshly. He can't see a thing, but he probably understands the situation better than anyone here. We're surrounded. We're outnumbered. Monnah is wounded, and as I study our group, I realize that Amluk is barely keeping himself standing. The poison is working its way through him.

Klatt-En addresses the boy. I don't understand much of what he says, though I know he's using several of the words for our weapons. The tone of his voice is diplomatic. Not at all anxious. I know now why he is one of the council members.

"What do they want?" I whisper.

"You," she says. "We're offering weapons and canoes instead."

The Kel-Ha-Nitika diplomat waits until Klatt-En finishes. Then he shakes his head deliberately. The Kel-Ha-Nitika *bwayna* raise their bows. They seem to be a word away from letting their arrows fly.

It's obvious they're not going to leave without me. There's no need for the rest of the Urah-wau to risk their own lives—not that I'm sure they would.

"I'll go with them," I say.

"No," says Sue.

"Awkye frey Kel-Ha-Nitika," I say loudly.

I'm trying to say that I'll go with the other tribe, but I don't really know my prepositions yet, so I'm just hoping I'm close.

Close enough, I guess, because the Urah-wau *bwayna* step aside to allow me to join the other tribe.

I enter the clearing that separates the Kel-Ha-Nitika from the Urah-wau. As I get closer to the enemy *bwayna,* I'm able to see farther back into the shadows. Now I know who the leader is. It's the tattooed warrior who tried to steal my computer.

Behind me, Sue begins shouting in her native language, attempting a last bit of negotiation. The outburst just seems to make the Kel-Ha-Nitika chief angry. He breaks into a rant. Semiformed

GREEN THUMB

words fly out of his mouth like meatballs, confusing even those who speak the language. His mouth is wide open, and I realize now why he uses the boy as his voice. His tongue is in the sack Sue carries with her. But even though the words are gibberish, his intention is clear. There will be no deal. They want me. And by the way his eyes flash and seem to bore right through me, I have no doubt that they are going to kill me.

I have to escape.

Remembering something Sue told me about the Indian's belief in the powers of white men, I widen my eyes, raise my arms skyward, and sonorously intone, as if I'm casting a spell: *"Kajagoogoo . . . oingo boingo . . . a-haaaaa! . . . wang chung, banarama, bow wow wow . . . !"*

As I continue my rhythmic recitation of MTV Mondo Retro mainstays, both groups of Indians slowly lower their weapons and stare at me in openmouthed consternation. It buys me the split second I need. I raise my *lit-zi* and blow it as hard as I can, giving the surrounding forest the command to shake. I spin, and tell the trees to drop fruit. Both tribes of Indians shrink back a bit as the trees react as if they've been hit by a monsoon. Bananas and softball-sized nuts rain to the ground, but I don't stick around to watch. I sprint.

Heading straight toward the leader, I wait until the last moment to change direction. I cut straight into the densest bit of jungle I can find

151

that leads me in the opposite direction of the Urah-wau. I scream in English, "RUN!" Then I blow the command for the branches, roots, bushes, and vines to part and allow me through. They oblige, and as I pass through I give the command to shut. Behind me I hear shouting, and I realize they've probably recovered from the initial surprise. I won't be able to outrun the Kel-Ha-Nitika *bwayna* for long, so I scramble up into one of the leafiest of trees, using my arms in the way I used to use the long leather belt. Bracing myself against the trunk twenty feet up the tree, I pull my blowgun out of my belt and load one of the poison-tipped darts. Within a couple seconds, one of my first pursuers cuts his way through the foliage. The dart sticks in his gut before he has a chance to take another step. He staggers and falls, but the next warrior is right behind him, and this one sees me. I've already got the dart in the blowgun, but my target ducks behind a tree trunk, and the dart sticks into the soft bark. He jumps out a moment later with his bow already drawn. I'm a sitting duck, but I blow two sharp high tones followed by two lengthy long ones, and the vine running up the tree winds its way around the arm drawing back his bowstring. The Indian screams, and the arrow flies wildly, hitting one of his tribesmen. The vine tightens its grip and actually pulls the screaming *bwayna* off the ground by the arm. All the noise is rallying the rest of the war party to my general vicinity. I can hear or see them coming from all angles. One of the closest ones is sprinting directly for the base of the tree I'm in, but as he passes one of the trees that separate us, I command one of the lowest branches to drop, effectively clotheslining the guy. He lands on his back and doesn't move.

I hear an arrow embed itself into the tree behind me before I feel it. I look down and see the tip buried deep in the tree and the friendly end quivering between my legs. The pain I don't notice until a second later. I see the blood streaming out of the back of my calf from a three-inch slice. Four short high notes later, a hanging vine swings into my hand. I grab ahold and leap from the tree just as two arrows stick in the spot I just vacated. The leap itself starts off like a bungee jump. I plummet straight down and I fear I'm going to break my legs landing on the jungle floor. But as the slack runs out, I begin arching back up toward the jungle ceiling. I repeat the command and just as I hit the pinnacle of my upswing, there's another vine waiting. This time, I try to be less a passenger and more a driver. Instead of just holding on for dear life, I lift my legs into a tight L shape like I'm on a swing, and I'm shooting for distance. I don't quite make it to the tree I'm hoping to reach, so I let go and fly the final ten feet, grasping for one of the thin branches. I grab on, and my momentum carries me all the way up over the branch like a gymnast preparing for a dismount. Managing to hold on, I scramble hand over hand back toward the trunk and drop myself down to a branch I can stand on.

The Kel-Ha-Nitika are in pursuit. One of the *bwayna* is attempting the same shortcut I took. He's got a vine in one hand and a machete in the other. He's swinging toward me. I whistle, and suddenly the branches supporting the vine simply "let go." I don't watch the fall, but I can't imagine that it's too pretty. I pull two darts from my pouch. I load the first into my blowgun, take aim, and fire. The nearest Indian grabs his thigh, takes two more steps, then collapses. The second Indian is Tongueless himself. He's nearly to the tree trunk when I let the next dart fly. It sticks into his chest, but he simply ignores it. He reaches the base of the tree and begins scrambling up, nimble and effortless as a monkey. I'm probably forty feet high, and I realize he'll reach me in a few seconds. The branch I'm standing on is thick, and that gives me an idea. I'm sure if I had longer to think about it, I wouldn't try this, but I have no time, so I'm able to act before fear paralyzes me. I sprint out away from the trunk on the branch. Just as it gets too thin to support my weight, I leap for the limbs of the next tree over. I catch a branch no more than two inches in circumference. It dips with my weight, and I'm able to grab a thicker branch. I scramble up onto it, then make my way again toward the center of the tree. Glancing back, I see Tongueless perched in the same spot I was moments before. He's eyeing the distance I just crossed. I blast out a command, and the thin branches of my tree bend upward. It's like lifting a drawbridge. Now there's no way he can make the same leap.

I use vines to cross distances my pursuers can't begin to keep up with, though I can still hear them shouting and moving as loudly as you'll ever hear an Indian in the jungle. I've doubled back now, and I'm heading in the direction of the Urah-wau village. I pause before swinging to a new tree. I realize I'm moving too fast. If I don't slow down, I'll lead the Kel-Ha-Nitika right back to the Urah-wau. With Monnah hurt and Amluk poisoned, the results would be disastrous. I reconsider my strategy for a moment. Inspiration comes again. I climb higher and higher into the tree until I'm probably a full hundred feet from the floor of the jungle. I command the nearby branches to fold up around me. Then I wait.

It proves to be excruciating, but before long the Kel-Ha-Nitika *bwayna* have caught up. They even assemble at the base of the tree I'm hiding in, though they don't see me. I catch occasional reflections off the blades of their machetes. I wonder if their justice is the eye-for-an-eye brand. From the tone of their shouting, I doubt they'll settle for my tongue. The *bwayna* split up and begin searching in different directions. I wait another five minutes, then begin swinging from tree to tree. I'm certain that Sue and the rest of the Urah-wau have made it back into the old jungle. A couple minutes later, I'm nearing the edge of the New Forest. I'm in the middle of a swing when, suddenly, I'm holding on to nothing. The ground rushes up at me. Mercifully I black out.

My eyes flutter open, and I see a figure above me. It's the teenaged interpreter, the spy I caught near the Urah-wau village. He's pulling back an arrow, and he's aiming it at my heart. Even in my semiconscious state, I can tell he's having doubts about what he's doing. His bow arm is trembling, and he can't really look me in the eye. I imagine this kill will make him a hero with his own tribe. He'll get over his guilt when the men are telling the story over the fire tonight. He pulls back the arrow. His eyes focus, then go glassy. He teeters for a moment. Just before he drops to the ground, I see the small globe of rubber pinned to his neck. The next voice I hear is urgent.

"Awkye!"

I roll my eyes to the side of my head. In the farthest periphery of my vision, I make out Anru. His normal grin is gone, and the look in his eye is a mixture of fear and concern. I see exactly what I'm expecting in his hand.

His blowgun.

*   *   *

Anru helps me up. He keeps hissing, "Hurry, Gray-ee, hurry!" We can hear others moving in the New Forest. I shake the cobwebs out of my head and follow Anru. He stops momentarily and picks something off the forest floor and shows it to me. It looks sort of like a boomerang without the curve. It's a flat, thin piece of wood. I take it from Anru's hand and run my hand over its surface. The edges have been sharpened into edges that resemble a serrated knife edge. Anru grunts, getting my intention. He takes the blade and pantomimes throwing it. With his hands, he shows a figure swinging a vine and the blade cutting through it. I catch his drift. The young Kel-Ha-Nitika used this to cut my vine in the middle of my swing. I stick the weapon in my belt as we leave the New Forest. We jog the few hundred yards to the safety of the old jungle. Just as we reach the tree line, Anru stops me. I'm not sure what he's doing as he turns me around. Then I feel a sharp pain in the kidney area. Anru holds up a dart that was stuck in my back. I don't even remember being hit. He holds up a "wait" finger and turns me back around. This time, the sting comes from my butt cheek. Anru holds up another dart. I've been shot twice. Anru points up the trail. "Hurry!" he says.

So we hurry.

*   *   *

We catch up to the rest of the party a few hundred yards outside of the village. I'm greeted with an entirely new respect. The *bwayna* are, on average, ten years older than me, but there's this look in their eyes, something between amazement and fear. When they last saw me I had a dozen Kel-Ha-Nitika warriors trying to kill me. Now I'm back and, other than a bleeding calf, I'm looking no worse for the experience. No one bothers to chastize Anru for secretly following the expedition. There are tears in Sue's eyes when she hugs me, but I initially mistake them for joy at seeing me alive. It takes me a moment to figure out that they're tears of sorrow. Over Sue's vibrating shoulder I see the limp figure carried by two of the larger *bwayna*.

Amluk is dead—killed by the poison fruit of the New Forest. There was nothing Ishoyla could do.

Even though I'm semi-immune to the curare poison of the darts, two full doses eventually slow me down. By the time we make it back to the village, I'm both thirsty and exhausted. I can barely keep my eyes open. Anru leads me into the hut where I've been sleeping. The last thing I remember is Sue coming in and washing my wound. I see her lips moving, but I'm too far gone to understand what she's saying.

I don't know how much later it is that I awaken. It's dark, however, and once again, the curare has left me with a killer headache and the feeling that my body, which should be about 75 percent water, isn't quite half right now. Some kind soul has left a pitcher by my cot though. I suck down the whole thing. I wander out of the hut and discover the village is deserted. I hear something coming from the riverbank, and I can see the glow of torchlight. I wander down to where it's coming from. The entire population of the village has gathered by the riverbank, and they're singing a song that sounds too happy for the occasion. Amluk's body has been tied down to a small raft and covered in some sort of shroud. The villagers hold candles, but they stand in line and, one by one, place the candles on the raft. When every villager has placed a candle, the singing stops. Klatt-En steps forward and throws a bit of dirt on the body. He says something I don't understand, and the raft is pushed away from the shore. The *bwayna* beat out a slow rhythm on the drums until the body is completely out of sight, and I'm left wondering why Sue and Kootah are missing.

The mystery is solved in the morning when Kootah comes staggering into the village. He's shouting and he stops right in the town center. I see Monnah exit his hut and walk out, then Klatt-En and Ishoyla. Soon, it seems, half the tribe is gathered around Kootah. I walk down the main path and stop when I'm standing alongside Anru. He does his best to translate what Kootah is saying.

The previous night, according to Anru, Kootah and Sue said their good-byes to their friend Amluk, then swore that they would avenge his death somehow. If the white scientists were responsible for the poison fruit that killed Amluk, then, Sue said, there was one way she knew she and Kootah could get even and save their jungle at the same time. So last night the two of them snuck into the camp. But when they entered one of the tents, a loud noise jumped out of a box. (At this point, I had to assume that Dr. Carter had gotten his hands on a motion detector alarm and set it in the lab.) Sue refused to run after the alarm sounded. She searched the tent, then stuffed something in Kootah's bag and something in her own. Then they ran. They managed to avoid the scientists coming out of the tents, then they split up at a spot where the trail forked. Moments later Kootah heard Sue shouting, then the voices of men, but it wasn't the language of the white man. It was Indian. Kootah doubled back. At the edge of the camp he watched as Sue was led back into camp by a war party of Kel-Ha-Nitika. Dr. Carter pointed out into the jungle and ordered the Indians to search for another. Kootah knew he had to move, but he stuck around long enough to see Dr. Carter sticking one of the needles that the white man uses to cure sickness into Sue. Sue collapsed, and Kootah ran the rest of the night to get back here this morning.

As Anru continues to translate, I notice that everyone has begun to stare at me. Kootah cuts through the crowd as he walks toward me and begins to open a pouch. Anru's words catch up with the action.

"Sue told me Awkye would know what to do with the *yulo*."

Kootah opens his pouch and pulls out the item that he and Sue risked their lives for. He hands the gray cartridge to me.

It's a battery for my laptop.

All Urah-wau eyes are on me, and they're all filled with expectation.

I plug the stolen battery into my laptop, which responds with a series of beeps as it comes to life. It doesn't take me long to locate the appropriate e-mail files. Dr. Carter kept up a steady stream of messages with a Dr. Aradillas in São Paulo and a Dr. Vandoley in Manhattan. I realize, when I see the date they're scheduled to arrive, that I have no idea how soon it will be, or if it's already happened. In fact, I haven't the slightest idea what the date actually is. Fortunately, my computer clock provides the answer. The representatives of the commission will arrive in thirty-six hours.

There's an immediate meeting of the tribal

council once I tell Monnah, via Anru, what I've learned. All of the tribe's *bwayna* are present. The pervading happiness of life within the Urahwau village is gone. Gloom clings to everyone: It's apparent in their expressions, in the way the villagers trudge from hut to hut, in the complete absence of music. Amluk is dead. Su-kay-waycha has been captured. Their homes, their way of life, will be bulldozed into oblivion—replaced by great ranches and poison forests. Monnah is the only speaker as the meeting begins, and as he exhorts his fellow Urah I sit wishing I spoke more of the language. Bits and pieces I understand, but most of it has to be translated, roughly, by Anru.

Monnah tells his fellow warriors that the Kel-Ha-Nitika's reputation for fierceness is undeserved, that they are violent, true, but that they are merely bandits who prey on the helpless and outnumbered. He reminds the others that their fathers had earned peace with the Kel-Ha-Nitika after continually defeating them in battle. He tells them that they have been hunting and fishing in peace for so long that it is time to call upon the warrior within each one of them.

"Remember," he says, "you will be fighting for your children and your children's children. And Su-kay-way-cha—she is daughter to us all."

I watch the faces of the assembled men. The power of the speech changes hopeless expressions to looks of resolve. A few of them begin to finger the edges of their machetes. Kootah, in particular, seems juiced. In fact, I'm afraid he'll simply sneak off in the night and undertake a suicide mission to avenge one friend's death and another's capture. Monnah begins suggesting a plan of attack, when one of the young *bwayna* abruptly bursts into the circle of men. He speaks so quickly and frantically that Anru doesn't bother translating right away. The news piques everyone's interest. I can tell by the way the men all lean forward and keep their eyes glued on the young scout. Finally, when he pauses, Anru updates me.

Loll, the scout, has returned from spying on the Kel-Ha-Nitika. He says finding them was simple. He followed the sound of *yulo*. I had trouble understanding what Anru was trying to say, because he was so excited. But after a couple attempts, using combinations of English and Indian words, he was able to tell me that the sound Loll heard came from chain saws. Because of the noise, Loll was able to sneak up to within thirty feet of where the Kel-Ha-Nitika were "killing the trees." It takes me a moment to figure out what they must be doing, but then it hits me. They're lengthening the road. Dr. Carter doesn't want to risk walking the committee members all the way through the jungle. He's probably afraid of ambush, or he fears the other scientists will notice the teeming life and all the noises of the jungle and somehow recognize the relative death of the New Forest. Another bonus of the strategy: It's normally an hour-and-a-half hike to the new forest. Once the road is complete, it'll be a fifteen-minute drive, albeit a bumpy one. The Kel-Ha-Nitika are probably getting to keep the chain saws, maybe Dr. Carter is even throwing in the truck.

"Tell Monnah the white men are making a path. They'll use the path to get to the New Forest in a truck," I tell Anru.

Anru spews out another combination of English and Urah-wau, but I clearly recognize the word "Toyota."

Monnah stands before saying a few final words. When he finishes, the *bwayna* disperse purposefully. I look at Anru.

"Monnah says we will stop them on the path."

For the rest of the night, preparations are made. Curare root is ground and mixed in tree sap. Rubber is separated from the trees and used to make more darts. The darts are dipped in the mixture of sap and poison. Machetes are sharpened. More arrows are cut. At midnight the drums come out, and while boys and women pound out a sharp rhythm, the men paint their faces with ochers and berry juices. The painting is different from the Kel-Ha-Nitika. Rather than the bands of black and red, the Urah-wau use alternating horizontal green and black inch-wide vertical stripes. The eye sockets are lined in red. I have to admit that, now, even the scrawniest of Urah-wau look fierce.

"Awkye!"

I turn as I hear my tribal name.

It's Monnah. He's pointing to a felled tree in front of him, indicating that I should sit. I do, and he reaches up toward my face with a gob of green goo in his fingers. He stops before he touches me, and asks the question with his eyes. I nod. He returns the gesture and begins to paint my face.

10

By morning, the thirty of us are perched hidden in the trees that line either side of the makeshift road cut by the Kel-Ha-Nitika. The original plan had been just to line up in the middle of the road and fire darts and arrows at the truck until it stopped. I had to convince Monnah that our weapons didn't have much of a chance to stop the four-wheel-drive vehicle, and that more than likely we'd just get run over. Besides, the last thing we needed to do was shoot one of the commission members. At the end of the day, those scientists and politicians had to believe us—me, specifically—rather than Dr. Carter, and our chances of that were much slimmer if one of their number had an arrow sticking out of him. There was some talk of chopping down a few trees and laying them across the road, but it was decided that the noise would attract the Kel-Ha-Nitika, and that would be a useless battle. Unless the prize—the commission—was actually there, it wasn't in our best interest to fight.

As we sit waiting in the trees, I finally have the time to consider my situation. Three months ago my biggest worry was my science project,

166

winning a trophy, turning my research into scholarships and grants. Being famous. I was a Dr. Carter in training, right down to my obsession with engineering every imperfection, every irregularity, every bit of random, unpredictable. . . *soul* out of nature. Now all I want to do is stop this man.

As I ponder the irony, I check the positions of my allies. Kootah is making me nervous. Last night, he spent the entire evening sharpening his machete in silence. Now he can't sit still like the rest of the Urah-wau. He keeps changing positions, and there's absolute hate in his eyes. He's ready to wreak some damage.

We hear the rumble of engines long before we see the blue of the pickup. All of us improve our hiding spots, ducking lower into the branches of the trees, freezing in place. Once the pickup is almost even with us, I see how the committee members are being transported. They're in a Hummer that's following the pickup. They must have put one on a barge sailing down the Amazon. The bed of the pickup is overflowing with Kel-Ha-Nitika *bwayna*. I count twelve. Sonja is driving the Toyota, and in the passenger seat I see my worst nightmare. Tongueless himself is riding shotgun. Jack is driving the Hummer, and I can see the crisp khaki of Dr. Carter's shirt next to him. He has his laptop open. He's probably boring the committee members with New Forest data. The next part of the plan is mine. When the vehicles are dead even with us, I blow into my *lit-zi*.

The rubber trees on either side of the path bend inward so low that the pickup is forced to come to a stop. At first, the Hummer honks, unaware of what the holdup is. We stay frozen in the trees. Our hope is that Dr. Carter and the rest of the commission will get out of the safety of their vehicle, but they don't. The experienced Kel-Ha-Nitika *bwayna* begin to scan the trees around them suspiciously. I'm watching Dr. Carter. I have a dart ready and I'm just waiting for him to set foot outside the Hummer. Instead, what he's doing seems strange. I can see his hands, and he's tapping away on his laptop, as if nothing is the matter. The tension of the moment is unnerving. Everyone just seems to be waiting for something to happen. The first sound is muffled. I look behind me and see that one of the younger Urah-wau has dropped his bow. The Kel-Ha-Nitika see it too. They begin shouting. That's all the signal needed. We let our first round of darts fly. I take aim at a tall, skinny *bwayna* sitting on the tailgate of the truck. My dart embeds itself into his thigh. In the first round of fire, four Kel-Ha-Nitika including mine crumple and fall. We've planned on a sort of shooting-gallery battle, so we have our dart pouches open on the branches next to us, but as I'm reaching for a second dart, something unbe-lievable happens. My tree begins to shake as if it's at the epicenter of an earthquake. It's almost as if *I* had commanded it to do so. I have no time to consider that though because I'm knocked out of my tree. I can hear the screams of my allies, also dropping like flies. I blow the *lit-zi* quickly and a vine comes to my hand and it swings me out to a spot a good ten yards behind the Hummer. Looking back on either side of the path, I see the results of the bucking and swaying of the trees. Most of the Urah-wau are on the ground. A few lucky ones, nearer the trunks or gripping smaller branches, have remained in the trees. The ones on the ground don't look good. Several have been knocked unconscious or worse. Loll, the young scout, manages to stand, but I can tell from here that his arm is broken. It's bent in a terribly unnatural way. The Kel-Ha-Nitika left standing are out of the pickup in a flash, raising their machetes and going after the dazed Urah-wau. I reach for a dart, before remembering that my dart pouch was resting next to me in the tree. It's gone now.

One of the Kel-Ha-Nitika warriors comes charging after me, carrying a machete. I whistle, and a root rises up from the ground and trips him. His chin lands at my feet. I pry the weapon out of his hand and smack him on the back of the head with the handle. Then I throw the weapon back into the jungle just in case he regains consciousness. I look up and I see one of the committee members staring back at me. His eyes and his mouth are wide open. I'm sure he's wondering what this teenaged, white American boy is doing outside his window fighting in what I'm sure Dr. Carter has convinced him is nothing more than tribal warfare. As I'm looking back toward the Hummer, the second surprising event of the battle takes place. The rubber trees that I commanded to bend low enough to stop the trucks are raising back up. I whistle, and they pause and begin to dip back into position, but a moment later they're upright again. Within seconds, the trucks will be able to drive straight out of here, making our stand futile.

I approach the back window of the Hummer and look inside. I can see Dr. Carter with the CB microphone pressed to the tiny speaker of his laptop.

So that's it. He's figured it out. He's taken my notes and now he knows the secret. I step up onto the bumper and look up on the roof. Mounted on top is a speaker. I climb all the way up, determined to disconnect it, but the vehicle starts moving almost as soon as I do. The Toyota is already past the rubber trees. Monnah, thrown in front of the Toyota when he was shaken out of the tree, has made it to his feet, but the truck accelerates, hits a stump, and pops a wheelie. My vision is blocked, but it looks like the cab lands right on him. The Wood Stock Project leaders are leaving their Kel-Ha-Nitika foot soldiers to fend for themselves. I look up in time to see Kootah withdrawing his bloody machete from the chest of one of the Kel-Ha-Nitika *bwayna*. He turns and sees the vehicles moving. I know who he's really after. He sprints straight at the Hummer like it's a game of chicken. When it's just a few feet from him, he jumps and lands spread-eagled on the hood. I wish I could see Dr. Carter's expression, but all I can see, directly in front of me, is Kootah. He rises to his knees and he's about to shatter the windshield with his weapon, when the crack of a gunshot does the job for him. A red penny-sized dot appears on Kootah's chest and his face is frozen in an expression of surprise. Streams of blood pour from the wound, and Kootah rolls unceremoniously off the hood of the vehicle.

The Hummer accelerates with me on top, leaving the battle behind us. I look behind me for Monnah's body, but see only Kootah writhing slowly on the ground.

It takes another fifteen minutes to make our way to the edge of the old forest. I've been scared to death that each time we hit a bump someone's going to hear my body thumping up here, and Dr. Carter will solve the problem by putting a bullet through the roof. But I don't roll off. This is our last chance. I wait until we hit the final row of trees, then I call down a vine, grab it, pull up, and let the Hummer roll out from under me.

I watch Jack pilot the vehicle over the quarter mile of wasteland. Figures exit both vehicles and assemble at the edge of the New Forest. I can imagine the "oooh"-ing and "my word"-ing taking place among the commission members. Some of them are probably calling it a miracle of science.

Yeah, like nuclear power.

I wait until they disappear into the blackness of the New Forest. Then I sprint out of the tree line and try to catch up. It takes me longer than it should, but it's because I run a zigzag pattern to throw off anyone who might be aiming an arrow at me. Finally I reach the spot where the cars are parked. I duck down behind the Hummer and catch my breath. Now I have to be quiet.

As soon as I enter the forest, I take to the trees. I can see more and move faster this way. After fifteen minutes or so of swinging out in widening circles, I finally hear something human. It's laughter. Carter is telling jokes less than an hour after killing a man. I climb down to the ground and creep up to their location as silently as I can. They still have Tongueless with them, and I'm fairly certain he, at least, hasn't been swept up in Dr. Carter's charm. He's alert.

The group is huddled in a tiny clearing in the heart of the New Forest. I can see why Carter brought them here. Some of the tallest enhanced trees are right in this spot. Plus, this is where he's planted his assortment of nonnative species, including the banana and orange trees. I notice that his laptop is open, and he's wearing it around his neck using a shoulder strap, like it's a guitar. The pistol still hangs in his belt holster. I slink in behind a thicket of smaller branches and vines and listen while he shares his vision of the future of the Amazon.

"Eventually the natives of the forest could harvest the crop for themselves and for profit. With the Amazon serving as the fruit bowl of the Southern Hemisphere, the Indians of the rain forest can become its newest tycoons."

Just what they want, I think. *Besides, get*

serious. They wouldn't have a chance. They would become the slaves of speculators and corporations.

"And none of this was here three years ago?" asks an incredulous committee member with a Portuguese accent.

"It was the desert you see surrounding it," Dr. Carter assures the man.

If the committee members were any more impressed, they'd be groveling at his feet. I notice Tongueless scanning the trees around them. That's a good sign. He isn't looking anywhere near me.

"Now take a deep breath," Dr. Carter says, demonstrating the procedure, opening his mouth wide and filling his lungs. The committee members begin doing as they're told. "You want to know why that's so satisfying?"

But before Dr. Carter can explain it to them, Tongueless grunts. I see him motion with his eyes in my direction, but he's looking up in the branches, not down on the ground where I am. I try to see what he's looking at. It takes me a moment to spot the movement. When I see it, I can't believe it.

Perched high in the tree next to the one I'm hiding behind and fumbling with a bow and arrow is Anru. My immediate fear is that Dr. Carter will simply pull out his gun and shoot him down, but I reconsider. How would that look in front of the committee—shooting a thirteen-year-old boy out of a tree? I keep my eyes glued to Dr. Carter. I see him nod almost imperceptibly at Tongueless. Then he simply keeps talking, though he's sort of lost his place. At the same time, he clicks around on his laptop. I know exactly what he's doing. He's going to "knock" Anru out of the tree. The boy will never survive a fall like that. I have no darts. Charging Dr. Carter would be suicide. Tongueless would chop me down before I made it three steps out of the tree line. Then they'd point to my war paint, and everyone would be sad, but they'd understand. The white boy made his decision and died for it.

But I have no choice. I take a step forward. Charging seems like a better option than just letting Anru die. He's saved my life, after all. But as I step, I feel something squish at my feet. It's a banana. One of the poison bananas of the New Forest. Now I have an idea.

As Dr. Carter fumbles with his controls while trying to maintain eye contact with his audience, Tongueless moves into the line of fire between Anru and Carter.

"Do you feel it?" Dr. Carter asks the group. "Come on. Take a deep breath. Suck in all that oxygen."

He demonstrates again. He opens his mouth wide, and the muscles in his chest rise. That's all I needed. I force a blast of air through my blowgun. The projectile flies out in a direct line toward Dr. Carter. It hits the back of his palate. Carter's mouth snaps shut reflexively, and I watch as his Adam's apple rises and falls. Dr. Carter's just gotten a taste of the fruit he created. The effects are immediate. Dr. Carter begins shuddering, and his eyes glaze over. With a shaky hand he punches one of the buttons on his laptop. The vines and brush that concealed me swing open, leaving me exposed. Dr. Carter points at me, but he's unable to muster a sound. He clutches his throat. None of the gawking spectators know how, but they suspect I'm responsible for Dr. Carter's condition.

Sonja is the first to speak. "Get him!" she screams at the Kel-Ha-Nitika warrior, but Tongueless doesn't need instruction. He has his own motivation, and he's covering the distance between the two of us in some haste. He's clutching a machete, and I somehow doubt he wants global warming explained to him.

A figure emerges out of the shadows and dives at the Kel-Ha-Nitika's legs just as he raises his blade, intent on giving me a haircut that I'm thinking is going to be way too short. The two go sprawling across the jungle floor. The new combatant is Monnah, caked in grease and dirt, his painted face looking like a chimney sweep's. He must have grabbed onto the underside of the pickup. Monnah's got one hand wrapped around Tongueless's machete wrist and the other around his throat. The Kel-Ha-Nitika recovers quickly from the surprise attack and manages to roll all the way over until he's on the top. He uses his free hand to dig his fingers into Monnah's shoulder wound. Monnah grimaces, but he won't give up his hold on the Kel-Ha-Nitika's wrist. I glance up into the tree and spot Anru with his bow drawn, but he can't risk a shot. A miss would more than likely nail Monnah. I'm about to jump on the pile when I notice Sonja tending to Dr. Carter, who has sunk to the ground. But she's not just comforting him. She's attempting to pull the gun from his holster. Unfortunately for her, she's standing underneath a dangling vine. I play three notes on the *lit-zi,* and the vine lowers and wraps around her neck. I instruct the vine to raise until Sonja is forced to stand on her tiptoes, her arms stretched above her, her hands clinging to the vine. Jack makes a run for Carter's gun, but he doesn't get more than three steps before an arrow lodges itself in his leg. He falls to the jungle floor screaming.

Monnah and Tongueless are still in a stalemate. Sweat pours from their bodies as they both refuse to let go of the machete, knowing that surrendering it will mean certain death. I make a split-second decision. Sprinting around the melee, I cross the thirty feet to the spot where Dr. Carter is struggling for breath. He's gasping out some word, but I don't have time for him right at this second. I reach into his holster and pull out the gun. I raise it above my head and fire. The explosion causes Tongueless to look up. What he sees is me. The barrel of the Smith & Wesson is leveled at him. He lets go of the machete, and it falls to the ground. Monnah scrambles up and picks up the weapon. He shouts something at Tongueless that I don't understand, but Tongueless evidently does. He lays down flat on his stomach.

For the first time since the battle began, I notice the committee members. They're gaping at me with just a bit of fear in their eyes. One of them even has his hands up like this is some kind of a stickup. Then I hear the sound. It's Dr. Carter. He's choking out a word. I lean closer.

"Ant . . . i . . . dote," he says.

"What antidote?" I say.

He looks up at Sonja and repeats the word.

"Do you have an antidote?" I demand.

But Sonja isn't in touch with reality.

"Antidote for what?" she gasps defiantly, wrestling with the vine around her neck.

"For the whole forest," I say. "For the poison fruit of these trees."

I instruct the tree to loosen its grip on Sonja so she can speak more clearly. She sneers. "There's nothing wrong with these trees or this forest. You're standing in the way of science here, Grady. It's perfected."

Dr. Carter begins hacking and going into a convulsion. I can also hear Jack whimpering behind me, but I'm confident that if he tries anything, Anru will let another arrow fly.

"You're letting him die," I say. "I'm guessing you're the only other person who knows the enhancement formula. Betcha that's a lucrative piece of information."

"Go back to junior high, Grady. Dissect some frogs."

I wander a few steps to my right and whistle. The banana tree lowers its branches down to me. I pull one off the bunch and begin peeling. I make my way quickly to Sonja.

"They're safe, huh?" I say.

"Go ahead. Eat one," she replies, but her defiant attitude has been shaken. She sees the writing on the wall.

"No," I say. "I think you should try one."

I rip off a chunk of banana and hold it up to her mouth. She stares at me with hate oozing from her every pore. She forces her lips shut as tightly as she can. The Wood Stock Project officially dies at that moment, but Dr. Carter's labored breathing makes it impossible for me to enjoy the moment.

"Where's the antidote, Sonja?"

She looks first to the committee members.

A tall one with an American accent snaps at her. "Tell him!"

She shakes her head and mutters. "It's in the glove box of the pickup."

I hand the gun to Monnah, then I'm gone. I

climb the nearest tree, then swing my way to the edge of the New Forest. I find a small vial just where Sonja said I would. I'm sure it doesn't take me longer than ten minutes to return, but as I swing down and land in the middle of the group, I know it's too late. Dr. Carter's eyes are wide open and dry.

All the healthy Urah-wau swarm over The Wood Stock Project camp shouting battle cries, prepared to annihilate Sue's captors, but there's a surprise waiting. By the time we descend on the tents, Sue's free. In fact, she has Francis tied up in a chair. Roddy's on the radio attempting to contact American authorities. Sue details how Roddy clocked Francis with a sack of coconuts after the others left in the morning.

"He told me he realized the day Dr. Carter shot at you that the man was crazy," she says. "After they captured me, Roddy snuck me extra food and told me jokes. When the others left to escort the commission to the New Forest, he set me free."

Roddy returns the radio microphone to its rack and faces me. "The embassy is going to send people to meet you at the airport in Belém. A barge is coming by tomorrow to pick up the commission members," he says. "They were awfully relieved to hear from us. Your mother has threatened most of the people in

Washington and São Paulo with lawsuits and bodily harm if you aren't returned soon."

There's a healthy amount of fear and respect for fire by those living in the jungle, but that night the Urah-wau start the largest contained blaze the Amazon has ever known—the entire New Forest. It doesn't survive the night. The commission members want Dr. Carter's body transported back to the United States for burial, but Monnah refuses. I can sort of understand his reason—not only the actual Indian words, but the meaning behind them.

"Yulo might bring him back."

If we can clone trees, mad scientists shouldn't be that much more difficult.

The tall American, the one named Vandoley, relents, not that he has much of a choice, and Dr. Carter is buried beneath the trees he brought to life. By morning, he lies under their ashes. Sue tells me about the fire. I miss it because I have things to do, and as much as I hate to admit it, part of me loved the New Forest, the fact that man could manipulate nature, force it to grow, make it strong.

So, even though it was an illusion, I wasn't anxious to watch it burn. Besides, I had my own fire to set. The first thing I did was gather all the computers, taking special note of Dr. Carter's, the one that held the secret to the plant language. This one I manually erase, using an ax I find nearby. I open up each unit and remove the hard drives, then I collect every floppy disk in the camp. Next, I gather all the files, notes, notebooks, printouts. After drenching all of it in gasoline, I set a match to three years of The Wood Stock Project's labor.

I do so right in front of Jack, Francis, and Sonja, who are guarded by Urah-wau *bwayna*.

"You can't turn back science," Sonja yells at me as the pile is engulfed in flame.

"I'm moving it forward," I say.

Even though they've defeated the Kel-Ha-Nitika, saved their forest home, and been reunited with their favorite daughter, the Urah-wau are in no mood to celebrate. They lost two men during the battle, and Kootah, in critical condition, has been flown to São Paolo for emergency treatment. Their mourning begins as soon as the New Forest is destroyed. I'm up half the night with the commission members showing them excerpts from Dr. Carter's notes still saved on my computer, and explaining to them the reasons the New Forest was a failure.

I must be quite a sight to them. I haven't had a haircut since I left the United States. And I'm still in war paint. I'm thirteen, and I'm telling them how their millions of dollars have been wasted.

Dr. Vandoley, who has been listening intently, finally speaks up. "But they were close, weren't they?" he asks. "After all, the data—which you say is correct—suggests arboreal species producing twice the oxygen, twice the usable wood in half the space. With some modifications, some tinkering—"

"Maybe," I say. "Maybe someone could make it work, but—"

"Yeah?" he says anxiously.

"Next time, if they're so sure it can be done, tell 'em to test it in their hometown."

Epilogue

On my first day of high school, Bobby Ross and Ed Stimmons try to remove my underwear the hard way. I resist vigorously, inflicting enough damage that when the punishments are handed out, I'm presumed to be the aggressor and get a full week of after-school detention compared to two days for Bobby and Ed. Mom, oblivious to all this, makes me take a box of homemade cookies to my "pal" Bobby's house. His sophomore sister, Elana, answers the door.

"So you're really in Bobby's class?" she says, giving me a slow, blatant, head-to-toe scan. "Hunh. Hard to believe."

"Uh, yeah. Look, my mom made these cookies for Bobby. Is he here?"

"Mm-hnh. But he doesn't want to see you." She takes the cookies anyway. "You didn't spit in them or anything, did you?"

"Nope. They're good. You should try one before you give them to Bobby."

"Maybe I'll try more than one," she says as she twists a long strand of blond hair around her finger. "Bobby can't taste anything with his nose busted up like that anyway."

"Just tell him I said I was sorry."

"Are you?" she asks. "I mean, I really hate to say this about my little brother, but let's face it: The guy's a dope."

I think about it for a moment. "No, I guess I'm not sorry. Not really."

Elana leans back against the door frame and arches her back. She tilts her head and fixes me with an expression that's sort of a bemused smirk but not exactly—not entirely. It's definitely a look no female has ever directed at me before.

"Did you really go to Northshores last year?" she said finally. "I think I would have remembered you."

I finish typing the details of my trip to the Ross household in my e-mail to Sue and hit "Send." Mom just called from downstairs. She's got the *Arsenic and Old Lace* video cued up, and Dad's back from picking up sushi.

I thought I was going to have so much free time after I decided to take a year off from science fair competition, but so far that hasn't been the case. The *L.A. Times* did a big story on The Wood Stock Project, so I've been getting interviewed a lot. Plus one of my lab partners called and invited me to one of his pool tournaments. I went—and got my butt kicked—but I had a good time. Then, last week, I read this thing in *Omni* about how there's this enzyme found in carrots that might actually slow Alzheimer's down a bit. The problem is that carrots produce so little of the enzyme, it isn't practical to manufacture the drug. But what if there were carrots that dripped with this enzyme? Anyway, I've just started checking out some books and looking into the research.

As I'm heading downstairs, I'm thinking that maybe someday I'll see Sue again. Maybe she'll go to BYU. Her adopted parents told her they'd send her if she wanted to when she got older.

I know it wasn't exactly my prerogative, but I made Dr. Carter's laptop a present to Sue—he *did* kidnap her after, all—along with one of the generators. So far we've written each other every couple days. Her first letters were mainly rambling stories about things she used to do with Amluk, and about how much she's missed him. Lately though she's begun to sound like she's beginning to cope. Kootah's recovery after treatment in São Paolo has lifted her spirits quite a bit. He should be back to normal in another month or so. Anru asks about me all the time. Sue says he flatly refuses to believe she can really talk to *Awkye* with the *yulo* box.

"He thinks you talk to trees, Grady," she wrote. "Isn't that priceless?"

Priceless?

Probably. It doesn't matter though. It's not for sale.